# HOW RAVEL ORCHESTRATED: MOTHER GOOSE SUITE

by
Peter Lawrence Alexander
Score Edited by Massimo Tofone

ALEXANDER PUBLISHING

Alexander Publishing
P.O. Box 1720
Petersburg, VA 23805
www.alexanderpublishing.com

Alexander Publishing is the
Publishing division of Alexander University, Inc.



Paperback edition published 2008
ISBN-13: 978-0-939067-12-1

Printed in the United States of America



Cover illustration by Caroline Alexander
Book design and layout by Caroline Alexander

Alexander, Peter Lawrence, 1950-

*To enhance your studies, the following optional tools are available from www.alexanderpublishing.com*

– *optional audio CD or MP3 download*
– *optional color coded study scores & separate PDF download of complete score.*

# CONTENTS

# INTRODUCTION

## The Composer In The Art Store

I wrote this book to alleviate the jealousy I was feeling every time I walked into an art store with my wife, or the graphics magazine section in Barnes and Noble. In either location, Caroline could find books or magazines on drawing mouths, smiles, eyes, hands, the anatomy, the brush strokes of Cezanne, the sketchbooks of Da Vinci, coloration and Degas, the Pre-Raphaelites, and on and on for literally hundreds of square feet. In the magazine section, there's row upon row of graphics magazines for all the programs which included tutorial upon tutorial upon tutorial!

Back over in the music book department I had the latest 28 rock biographies, the third edition of the *Harvard Dictionary of Music*, 263 different guitar books (with pictures), the occasional Dover score and...that's about it. So, off to the magazine racks. There are tons of music magazines mostly dedicated to rock, one or two on jazz, a couple on drums, recording, and of course the few publications that deal with music production software.

But no brush strokes. No smiles. No coloration. No neat and cool tutorials for writing music like Caroline was finding for creating art in Photoshop and 3D software.

So back to the table we sit, each with our own *Café Mocha*.[1] For upwards of two hours I hear my wife say things like, "Coool. Oh. Wow. Ahhh, so *that's* how he did that!" And so on.

By comparison, my music magazines read like a tech manual for GE's newest jet engine. No brush strokes there. I leave the table to wander around hoping I'll find something to feed *my* art and craft. After half an hour of wandering, the only thing I find that mildly interests my creativity is *Stupid Yo-Yo Tricks*.[2]

Having had enough of that, I look for the newest *Spenser For Hire* book by Robert B. Parker and meander back to the table. I finish my *Café Mocha*. Read. Stare at the cheesecake selections. Read some more. Look at the 10 or 12 different varieties of Starbucks coffee cups. Finally, it's time to go. As we check out, Caroline has a stack of useful magazines on her craft, and I've got a paperback about shooting someone in Las Vegas.[3]

---

[1] Venti's in case you're curious, or for historical reasons - should this book still be around in a hundred years.
[2] *Not* a book by the cellist Yo-Yo Ma on the quirky things you can do with a cello bow.
[3] What happens there, stays there.

After a few years of this, I decided to do something about this dilemma for composers that would be a good read and a good listen. And here it is, *How Ravel Orchestrated: Mother Goose Suite*. [4]

## A First in Many Ways

*How Ravel Orchestrated: Mother Goose Suite* is a first in a many ways. To start with, I had a brand new music engraving done of the entire score with the piano part at the bottom, so that now you can see:

1. How Ravel transcribed his own piano work for orchestra (a class in itself)
2. And, well, how Ravel orchestrated!

Next, we licensed both an optional CD and MP3 performance of the complete work that you can order from the www.alexanderpublishing.com website. Also available is a complete performance of the Mother Goose Suite on YouTube - which you can view at www.alexanderpublishing.com.

Also available from www.alexanderpublishing.com are duplicate copies of the score in downloadable PDF format including a special color-coded PDF edition highlighting how Ravel orchestrated from piano to full orchestra.

The idea behind this is portable learning. So whether with your MP3 player, your CD player, your car stereo, the CD player in your computer, or even an iPhone - which can view video, you can learn just about anywhere you want.

Even if you have weak music reading or score reading skills, this practical application of technology opens great doors for you.

## The Stories Behind the Music

To confess, I haven't spent much time with Mother Goose stories now that my children are grown. So you can imagine my surprise to discover that these weren't nursery rhymes, but full length, and in places, very gritty stories. After reading a few, I decided to include the story that was the background for each piece. Doing this created an enormous payoff.

As someone who spent over 20 years in Los Angeles with many hours on the scoring stage, after reading the stories and comparing them to the score, I was pleasantly surprised to discover how cue-like Ravel's music is. Since each suite represents a specific story, or portion of a story, you actually have five mini problem/solution case studies for scoring specific dramatic elements. You'll find the full range of dramatic, romantic and comedic writing in *Mother Goose Suite*. In fact, every compositional technique used by Ravel, you'll find in the film scores of Jerry Goldsmith, John Williams and many others.

---

[4] First in a series.

## Analysis For the Working Composer

First the story, then the score, then the orchestration analysis. To create an analysis that would manage your time well, be interesting to read, yet practical, I started by having the score engraved with bar numbers at page bottom. This allows for quick and easy referencing.

The optional colorized PDF score also speeds the learning curve, because you can quickly look things up and glance at the colorized score to get what you need.

## Jazz, Baby

There are places where I've looked at Ravel's harmonic vocabulary. When I did this, I used the standard jazz/pop music notation citing the chord symbol, altered tones, pitch in the bass, and where applicable, chord scales (modes). To make this as accessible as possible, there's no figured bass.

When going through the score, especially *The Dialog of Beauty and The Beast*, one must be impressed by the way Ravel absorbed the jazz language he was learning in the Parisian nightclubs, and made it his own in a concert environment. Through jazz/pop harmony eyes, you see his use of altered dominant chords, the altered Mixolydian scale, polytonality, and triads with the added $9^{th}$, to name a few innovations.

By knowing the story, the lessons from Ravel are enhanced as we see how he combined harmony and orchestration to support the story dramatically.

## From the Piano to the Orchestra

We learn an important lesson from Ravel: what you write for piano and what for orchestra are two different things. As a professional writer, you should look at the piano and the orchestra, each as two totally different performance media. To translate from piano  to the orchestra is like translating from book to stage or book to movie. How you can explain in a book is one thing, how you tell a story and visualize for the screen or for the stage is something entirely since each has its demands and limitations for story telling.

You can see Ravel's thinking. "I've written this work for the piano. Now I have a full orchestra to work with. How do I orchestrate and recompose to take full advantage of the that medium?" With this approach, Ravel felt total freedom to change as needed with his own music.

When it was the music of another composer, he made few changes to the piano part, wanting to keep to the composer's original intent. In your own writing, you'll have to make similar choices.

## French to Italian

Purists may disagree with my choice, but because we're more accustomed to working with Italian musical terms than French, we translated the French into Italian. In some cases, we wrote the performance instruction in English because we felt that more conveyed Ravel's instructions. I also did this for copyright purposes to clearly establish our ownership of the re-engraved score.

## Score Layout

The score faithfully follows the original Durand edition of Mother Goose Suite, with this one difference: for study and note taking purposes there is only one (1) orchestral system per page. Thus, some pages will look a little empty, but for a student, I think our layout approach is much easier to work with. The book is laid out so that the first page of the score is always on the left page. This lets you see two pages at once.

## How Ravel Worked

Following this introduction, I have a short section detailing the working methods of Ravel. I think you'll find this useful in seeing how Ravel developed his craft.

## The Influence of Edgar Allan Poe

After the five suites, I've included two major works written by Edgar Allan Poe that clearly impacted Ravel and his art. The first is called *The Poetic Principle*. The second is called *The Philosophy of Composition*.

Both of these are, again, good reads. And their inclusion gives us a more complete picture of the man and how he approached his craft. Ravel's music wasn't just impacted by other musical works, it was touched and influenced by art (*Pictures At An Exhibition*), story (*Mother Goose Suite, The Child and The Magic, Scheherazade*), machinery (*Bolero*, which was written to musically imitate a machine), and poetry (*Three Poems* by Stephen Mallarme).

## Finale

My prayer is that this work will be blessing and a joy that adds to your learning.

*Peter Lawrence Alexander*
*Petersburg, Virginia*
*October 2008*

# How Ravel Worked

The information in this section is from Roger Nichols' *Ravel Remembered,*[1] which unfortunately, is permanently out of print. Rather than summarize these observations, I thought it would be better to let those who knew Ravel and how he worked, have their own voice.

### Marguerite Long (1878-1966)

Ravel's integrity and loyalty were beyond reproach.[2]

### Roland-Manuel

His general culture, which was exquisite without being particularly broad, had given him exactly the right materials to suit his aesthetic, providing Baudelaire as his friend and counselor and, through Baudelaire, Edgar Allan Poe[3] – the Poe of *The Poetic Principle* and *The Philosophy of Composition*.[4]

## Composing

### Edmond Maurat

**Ravel:** I don't have ideas. To begin with, nothing forces itself on me.

**Maurat:** But if there's no beginning, how do you follow it all up? What do you write down first of all?

**Ravel:** A note at random, then a second one and, sometimes, a third. I then see what results I get by contrasting, combining and separating them. From these various experiments there are always conclusions to be drawn; I explore the contents and developments of these. These half-formed ideas are built up automatically; I then range and order them like a mason building a wall. As you see, there's nothing mysterious or secret in all this.[5]

---

1 Roger Nichols, *Ravel Remembered*, Copyright © 1987 by Roger Nichols, originally published by Faber and Faber Limited, 3 Queen Square London, WC1N 3AU

2 Ibid, page 32

3 Both works are in this volume.

4 Ibid, page 143

5 Ibid, page 55

### Conversation With Robert de Fragny

The G major Concerto took two years of work, you know. The opening theme came to me on a train between Oxford and London. But the initial idea is nothing. The work of chiseling then began. We've gone past the days when the composer was thought of as being struck by inspiration, feverishly scribbling down his thoughts on a scrap of a paper. Writing music is seventy-five per cent an intellectual activity. This effort is often more pleasant for me than having a rest.[6]

### Manuel Rosenthal

The first time I went to see him after he became ill, there were some manuscripts lying on the piano and I asked his permission to look at them. He said sadly, 'Oh well, now you can, because I'm not going to go with that composition.' And to my astonishment I could see that it looked like any composition by Bach or Mozart: a melodic line with a figured bass, and only when he couldn't figure the chords he'd had to write them out. But it was very simple, written on two or three staves, no more.[7]

## Orchestration

### Louis Aubert (1877-1968)

In the days when we were both in Faure's composition class we lived closed to each other and that was a further bond between us. Often, right at the end of the evening, our family gathering would be startled by a ring at the door, and someone would say: 'Ah! It's Ravel.' He might for instance, have come to discuss some detail in writing for the harp, an instrument one of my sisters played. There was no instrument that he had not studied as thoroughly as was possible, and he pursued this knowledge with the single-mindedness of a man possessed by an exclusive passion.[8]

### Helene Jourdan-Morhange

During the week Ravel sometimes worked for several nights on end. When he was writing his Sonata for violin and piano he would often ask me to come over to put in fingerings and bowings.[9]

### Manuel Rosenthal, Ravel Defines Orchestration

I had been studying with him for some time and he kept repeating, 'You still don't understand orchestration. This is only instrumentation.' Then I finally brought him a score and he said, 'Ah! Now that's orchestration.'

'But what's the difference?' I asked

'Instrumentation,' he said, 'is when you take the music you or someone else has written and you find the right kind of instruments – one part goes to the oboe,

6 Ibid, page 61
7 Ibid, page 61
8 Ibid, page 11
9 Ibid, page 122

another to the violin, another to the cello. They go along very well and the sound is good but that's all. But orchestration is when you give a feeling of the two pedals at the piano: that means that you are building an atmosphere of sound *around* the music, around the written notes – that's orchestration.[10]

### Arbie Orenstein

Ravel stressed the importance of the piano and the string family. When orchestrating, he felt the need to isolate the notes of each family of instruments at the keyboard and observe, for example, what the woodwinds were doing at a particular moment.. Most of his tutti are organized by families of instruments, which gives a full yet clear resonance. Ravel considered the strings the soul of the orchestra and generally notated their parts before the other instruments. He insisted that the string family sound perfectly in and of itself, and once this task was accomplished, the final choice of instrumentation would be made. In the course of a lesson, Manuel Rosenthal was shown the original version of the "Pavane" from *Ma Mere L'Oye*, which was notated solely for the string family.[11]

### Madeleine Grey (1897 - 1979)

He was terribly demanding to work with, because his scores left nothing to chance.[12]

## Listening to New Works of Other Composers

### Tristan Klingsor (1874-1966)

In our own gathering of artists it was the painter Paul Sordes who did the talking; Ravel was the dreamer. If some new work had to be sight-read, it was Sordes who sat down at the piano; Ravel listened without moving. He was comparing, inwardly analyzing and, while appearing to be idle, working and immersing himself even more deeply in the magical, mathematical world of music.[13]

## From One Who Contracted Ravel to Compose

### Mikhail Fokine (1880-1942) On Ravel's Composing *Daphnis and Chloe*

Total freedom in creation – freedom in choice of musical form, measure, and rhythms, and in the length of the individual parts – gave him a joyful opportunity to begin his composition of the music, a task which, under former conditions, most composers had shunned.[14]

---

[10] Ibid, page 67-68

[11] Arbie Orenstein, *Ravel Man and Musician*, Copyright © 1991 by Arbie Orenstein, originally published by Dover Publications, Inc., 31 East 2nd Street, Mineola, NY 11501

[12] Ibid, page 84

[13] Ibid, page 14

[14] Ibid, page 43

# The Eight Keys To Learning Professional Orchestration

When it comes to looking at orchestration and orchestral devices, there has arisen a mistakenly dangerous chatter among novices that learning these devices is for "classical music" or "symphonic music" only. Far from it. As a writer, an orchestra is another ensemble that has principles of writing for just as there are principles of writing for jazz big band.

The principles that I teach in *Professional Orchestration* or *Writing For Strings* are independent of music style. You can apply these principles to "concert music" or film or arrangements for vocalists, etc. Instruments "speak" different colors in different registers and in the various combinations, also called devices. The writing objective is to take these techniques, apply them to various styles, and see what works best. You can find violins in unison or octaves in a Country Music ballad, a film cue, a video computer game, or in Ravel! So don't limit yourself to thinking these combinations are for only one style of music!

To be successful, you have to know about 1000 orchestral devices, all of which are easily learnable. We begin learning these combinations by applying the *8 Keys to Learning Professional Orchestration*. Here they are:

1. Seeing how the melody is handled with solo instruments
2. Seeing how the melody is treated within each orchestral section
3. Seeing how the melody is treated by combining orchestral sections
4. Seeing how the melody is harmonized with three or more parts in each orchestral section
5. Seeing how the melody is harmonized with three or more parts by combining orchestral sections
6. Solving practical scoring issues
7. Writing for voice and orchestra
8. Writing for voice

To make the *Eight Keys* work, you question the music. When we do that with *Mother Goose Suite*, we immediately omit Keys 7 and 8 because it's an all instrumental work.

## 1) Seeing How the Melody Is Handled With Solo Instruments

Initially, you want to ask nine questions of the movement (or cue if it's a film score):

1. Is the melody (or counterline) assigned to one instrument only, or is the melody passed to other solo instruments phrase by phrase?
2. Which solo instruments are used?
3. In what register are they placed: low, medium, high, very high, across registers, leaps?
4. What's the dynamic level?
5. What other instruments in the orchestra are also playing? What is their dynamic level? In what register?
6. Is the melody passed from a solo instrument to an orchestral section? If yes, what section and what is the effect on the listener?
7. If the melody is passed from a solo instrument to an orchestral section, does it go back to a solo instrument? If yes, which one(s) and what is the effect on the listener?
8. How long in minutes (or SMPTE timecode) is the movement?
9. What is the form of the movement or piece or song?

The first few times you do this, it can seem a bit cumbersome, but over time it gets to be second nature.

## 2) Seeing How the Melody Is Treated Within Each Orchestral Section

The *Second Key* begins to open up dozens of possible combinations for melodic presentation. In *Professional Orchestration Volume 2, Orchestrating the Melody Within Each Orchestral Section,* there are 56 different combinations for the strings alone that are either unison for each section or two parts in octaves, three parts in three octaves, etc. Within each section there are also thirds and sixths.

## 3) Seeing How the Melody Is Treated by Combining Orchestral Sections

The *Third Key* leads us to understand the who, what, where, why, when and how of unison and octave doublings with combined sections. The Third Key totally expands your palette of colors because here: combining orchestral sections can be one or more sections combined; a solo instrument combined with a section; or several solo instruments combined with one or more sections. In jazz writing, these are called *doublings* or *devices*. In MIDI terminology, it's called *layering*.

## 4) Seeing How the Melody Is Harmonized With Three or More Parts in Each Orchestral Section

The *Fourth Key* is about 3-4 part vertical harmony within each section. With the brass and strings, we can expand that to seven- and eight-part harmony depending on the ensembles you have to work with. Depending on your writing background, it's at this point that struggles can begin on understanding how to voice each section, and with the strings, how to set up effective divisi writing.

With the woodwind section, there are two standard setups: the classical setup by pairs (2 flutes, 2 clarinets, 2 oboes, 2 bassoons); and the Wagnerian section with three of each. Each has its own way of effective voicing within the section.

With the brass section, you have trumpets, trombones and French horns. A smaller section can be 3, 3 and 3. A larger section can have three trumpets, three trombones and tuba, and four French horns.

Each instrument within each section has its own range. Each section as a whole has its own effective range.

How you voice and harmonize within each section gives you different shades and colors, and with strings and brass, this is enhanced with the use of muting.

A serious consideration within the Fourth Key is looking at these vertical structures to see which chord tones were doubled.

## 5) Seeing How the Melody Is Harmonized With Three or More Parts by Combining Orchestral Sections

Borrowing from jazz writing, the *Fifth Key* is what's commonly called *doubling*. If you looked at a big band arrangement, you might see, "*Flute 1 col Tpt 1*." This means that Flute 1 is doubling Trumpet 1 in the same register. You might see, "*Flute 1 col Tpt 1 8va*." This means Flute 1 is doubling Trumpet 1 an octave higher in a different register. Depending on the writer, you sometimes see this on a film score. But on a full orchestral score, it's always written out. So the question is, "What do you double and when?" There are no "rules" for this, but there is common practice. And within common practice there's the stylistic consideration of the individual composer's style, along with the kind of music being written. From a dramatic scoring perspective, what you're determining is the effect you're trying to create.

## 6) Solving Practical Scoring Issues

These include: tutti passages of the whole orchestra; combined sections; or a single section; *sforzando-piano*; *piano-sforzando*; repetition of phrases; imitation; echo; emphasizing certain notes and chords; crescendo and diminuendo, etc.

### 7) Writing For Voice and Orchestra

This isn't a factor with *Mother Goose*, but for completeness, this includes: the kind of ensemble used; doubling voices within the orchestration; handling recitatives; accompanying the chorus; the solo voice and ensemble.

### 8) Voices

Briefly, this covers: the voices selected; the lyrics; voice colors; combining voices; trios; quartets; and chorus.

## More Than a Framework, Your Personal Mentor

You can look at the *8 Keys to Learning Professional Orchestration* as a framework for study, and that would be valid. But, if you take them to heart and learn to use these with each piece you studio, they become your Personal Mentor.

### The 8 Keys and Ravel

Since there are no vocals, we'll use six of the 8 Keys as our method for studying *How Ravel Orchestrated: Mother Goose Suite*.

Your printed score contains the complete 4-hand piano parts merged as one. Besides dynamic and pianistic effects translated to the orchestra, look at piano phrasing vs. string bowings to see what Ravel did, then compare the piano to the orchestra.

## Order of Study

To get the most out of *How Ravel Orchestrated: Mother Goose Suite* go through these steps:

1. Read the story first
2. Check the notes on each piece to see which part of the story Ravel composed for
3. Listen to the orchestra on the optional audio
4. Replay the movement, and as best as possible, conduct as you score read (you'll be amazed how much more you pick up when you're trying to conduct)
5. Mark the score to see which instruments were assigned to the various lines, and in a notebook, write down what you're seeing, based on the *8 Keys of Professional Orchestration*
6. Download the optional colorized PDF score and print it out. See how the piano part was translated to the orchestra
7. Reduce the orchestration down to 4-staves and compare to the piano part
8. Apply to your own writing.

## What About MIDI Mock-ups?

If you're working with electronic scoring, as many of us now have to, this is the time to check your sample libraries, piece by piece, and see what colors you have available. For example, in bar 5 of *Pavane for The Sleeping Princess*, the first half note in the Harp is a D4 while the second is a harmonic for the D written an octave lower but sounding an octave higher. Does your sampled harp have harmonics? Do you get the same coloration as you hear in the orchestra? Bar 17 - viola harmonics. Do your libraries have that? If yes, how do the sampled viola harmonics sound compared to the live orchestra?

Of course, you can also do a MIDI mock-up of this piece, and that's a great way to build skills. But use the opportunity that samples give you to experiment. Staying with *Pavane*, from bars 1 to 8, the melody is given to the flute. How would the piece change if you gave the melody to the oboe instead? Question, experiment, learn.

# The Sleeping Beauty In The Woods

## A Story by Charles Perrault

### *From "Contes du temps passé", (1697)*

Once upon a time there lived a king and queen who were grieved, more grieved than words can tell, because they had no children. They tried the waters of every country, made vows and pilgrimages, and did everything that could be done, but without result. At last, however, the queen found that her wishes were fulfilled, and in due course she gave birth to a daughter.

A grand christening was held, and all the fairies that could be found in the realm (they numbered seven in all) were invited to be godmothers to the little princess. This was done so that by means of the gifts which each in turn would bestow upon her (in accordance with the fairy custom of those days) the princess might be endowed with every imaginable perfection.

When the christening ceremony was over, all the company returned to the king's palace, where a great banquet was held in honor of the fairies. Places were laid for them in magnificent style, and before each was placed a solid gold casket containing a spoon, fork, and knife of fine gold, set with diamonds and rubies. But just as all were sitting down to table an aged fairy was seen to enter, whom no one had thought to invite - the reason being that for more than fifty years she had never quitted the tower in which she lived, and people had supposed her to be dead or bewitched.

By the king's orders a place was laid for her, but it was impossible to give her a golden casket like the others, for only seven had been made for the seven fairies. The old creature believed that she was intentionally slighted, and muttered threats between her teeth.

She was overheard by one of the young fairies, who was seated nearby. The latter, guessing that some mischievous gift might be bestowed upon the little princess, hid behind the tapestry as soon as the company left the table. Her intention was to be the last to speak, and so to have the power of counteracting, as far as possible, any evil which the old fairy might do.

Presently the fairies began to bestow their gifts upon the princess. The youngest ordained that she should be the most beautiful person in the world; the next, that she should have the temper of an angel; the third, that she should do everything with wonderful grace; the fourth, that she should dance to perfection; the fifth, that she should sing like a nightingale; and the sixth, that she should play every kind of music with the utmost skill.

It was now the turn of the aged fairy. Shaking her head, in token of spite rather than of infirmity, she declared that the princess should prick her hand with a spindle, and die of it. A shudder ran through the company at this terrible gift. All eyes were filled with tears.

But at this moment the young fairy stepped forth from behind the tapestry.

"Take comfort, your Majesties," she cried in a loud voice; "your daughter shall not die. My power, it is true, is not enough to undo all that my aged kinswoman has decreed: the princess will indeed prick her hand with a spindle. But instead of dying she shall merely fall into a profound slumber that will last a hundred years. At the end of that time a king's son shall come to awaken her."

The king, in an attempt to avert the unhappy doom pronounced by the old fairy, at once published an edict forbidding all persons, under pain of death, to use a spinning wheel or keep a spindle in the house.

At the end of fifteen or sixteen years the king and queen happened one day to be away, on pleasure bent. The princess was running about the castle, and going upstairs from room to room she came at length to a garret at the top of a tower, where an old serving woman sat alone with her distaff, spinning. This good woman had never heard speak of the king's proclamation forbidding the use of spinning wheels.

"What are you doing, my good woman?" asked the princess.

"I am spinning, my pretty child," replied the dame, not knowing who she was.

"Oh, what fun!" rejoined the princess; "how do you do it? Let me try and see if I can do it equally well."

Partly because she was too hasty, partly because she was a little heedless, but also because the fairy decree had ordained it, no sooner had she seized the spindle than she pricked her hand and fell down in a swoon.

In great alarm the good dame cried out for help. People came running from every quarter to the princess. They threw water on her face, chafed her with their hands, and rubbed her temples with the royal essence of Hungary. But nothing would restore her.

Then the king, who had been brought upstairs by the commotion, remembered the fairy prophecy. Feeling certain that what had happened was inevitable, since the fairies had decreed it, he gave orders that the princess should be placed in the finest apartment in the palace, upon a bed embroidered in gold and silver.

You would have thought her an angel, so fair was she to behold. The trance had not taken away the lovely color of her complexion. Her cheeks were delicately flushed, her lips like coral. Her eyes, indeed, were closed, but her gentle breathing could be heard, and it was therefore plain that she was not dead. The king commanded that she should be left to sleep in peace until the hour of her awakening should come.

When the accident happened to the princess, the good fairy who had saved her life by condemning her to sleep a hundred years was in the kingdom of Mataquin, twelve thousand leagues away. She was instantly warned of it, however, by a little dwarf who had a pair of seven-league boots, which are boots that enable one to cover seven leagues at a single step. The fairy set off at once, and within an hour her chariot of fire, drawn by dragons, was seen approaching.

The king handed her down from her chariot, and she approved of all that he had done. But being gifted with great powers of foresight, she bethought herself that when the princess came to be awakened, she would be much distressed to find herself all alone in the old castle. And this is what she did.

She touched with her wand everybody (except the king and queen) who was in the, castle-governesses, maids of honor, ladies-in-waiting, gentlemen, officers, stewards, cooks, scullions, errand boys, guards, porters, pages, footmen. She touched likewise all the horses in the stables, with their grooms, the big mastiffs in the courtyard, and little Puff, the pet dog of the princess, who was lying on the bed beside his mistress. The moment she had touched them they all fell asleep, to awaken only at the same moment as their mistress. Thus they would always be ready with their service whenever she should require it. The very spits before the fire, loaded with partridges and pheasants, subsided into slumber, and the fire as well. All was done in a moment, for the fairies do not take long over their work.

Then the king and queen kissed their dear child, without waking her, and left the castle. Proclamations were issued, forbidding any approach to it, but these warnings were not needed, for within a quarter of an hour there grew up all round the park so vast a quantity of trees big and small, with interlacing brambles and thorns, that neither man nor beast could penetrate them. The tops alone of the castle towers could be seen, and these only from a distance. Thus did the fairy's magic contrive that the princess, during all the time of her slumber, should have nought whatever to fear from prying eyes.

At the end of a hundred years the throne had passed to another family from that of the sleeping princess. One day the king's son chanced to go a-hunting that way, and seeing in the distance some towers in the midst of a large and dense forest, he asked what they were. His attendants told him in reply the various stories which they had heard. Some said there was an old castle haunted by ghosts, others that all the witches of the neighborhood held their revels there. The favorite tale was that in the castle lived an ogre, who carried thither all the children whom he could catch. There he devoured them at his leisure, and since he was the only person who could force a passage through the wood nobody had been able to pursue him.

While the prince was wondering what to believe, an old peasant took up the tale.

"Your Highness," said he, "more than fifty years ago I heard my father say that in this castle lies a princess, the most beautiful that has ever been seen. It is her doom to sleep there for a hundred years, and then to be awakened by a king's son, for whose coming she waits."

This story fired the young prince. He jumped immediately to the conclusion that it was for him to see so gay an adventure through, and impelled alike by the wish for love and glory, he resolved to set about it on the spot.

Hardly had he taken a step towards the wood when the tall trees, the brambles and the thorns, separated of themselves and made a path for him. He turned in the direction of the castle, and espied it at the end of a long avenue. This avenue he entered, and was surprised to notice that the trees closed up again as soon as he had passed, so that none of his retinue were able to follow him. A young and gallant prince is always brave, however; so he continued on his way, and presently reached a large forecourt.

The sight that now met his gaze was enough to fill him with an icy fear. The silence of the place was dreadful, and death seemed all about him. The recumbent figures of men and animals had all the appearance of being lifeless, until he perceived by the pimply noses and ruddy faces of the porters that they merely slept. It was plain, too, from their glasses, in which were still some dregs of wine, that they had fallen asleep while drinking.

The prince made his way into a great courtyard, paved with marble, and mounting the staircase entered the guardroom. Here the guards were lined up on either side in two ranks, their muskets on their shoulders, snoring their hardest. Through several apartments crowded with ladies and gentlemen in waiting, some seated, some standing, but all asleep, he pushed on, and so came at last to a chamber which was decked all over with gold. There he encountered the most beautiful sight he had ever seen. Reclining upon a bed, the curtains of which on every side were drawn back, was a princess of seemingly some fifteen or sixteen summers, whose radiant beauty had an almost unearthly luster.

Trembling in his admiration he drew near and went on his knees beside her. At the same moment, the hour of disenchantment having come, the princess awoke, and bestowed upon him a look more tender than a first glance might seem to warrant.

"Is it you, dear prince?" she said; "you have been long in coming!"

Charmed by these words, and especially by the manner in which they were said, the prince scarcely knew how to express his delight and gratification. He declared that he loved her better than he loved himself. His words were faltering, but they pleased the more for that. The less there is of eloquence, the more there is of love.

Her embarrassment was less than his, and that is not to be wondered at, since she had had time to think of what she would say to him. It seems (although the story says nothing about it) that the good fairy had beguiled her long slumber with pleasant dreams. To be brief, after four hours of talking they had not succeeded in uttering one half of the things they had to say to each other.

Now the whole palace had awakened with the princess. Every one went about his business, and since they were not all in love they presently began to feel mortally hungry. The lady-in-waiting, who was suffering like the rest, at length lost patience, and in a loud voice called out to the princess that supper was served.

The princess was already fully dressed, and in most magnificent style. As he helped her to rise, the prince refrained from telling her that her clothes, with the straight collar which she wore, were like those to which his grandmother had been accustomed. And in truth, they in no way detracted from her beauty.

They passed into an apartment hung with mirrors, and were there served with supper by the stewards of the household, while the fiddles and oboes played some old music and played it remarkably well, considering they had not played at all for just upon a hundred years. A little later, when supper was over, the chaplain married them in the castle chapel, and in due course, attended by the courtiers in waiting, they retired to rest.

They slept but little, however. The princess, indeed, had not much need of sleep, and as soon as morning came the prince took his leave of her. He returned to the city, and told his father, who was awaiting him with some anxiety, that he had lost himself while hunting in the forest, but had obtained some black bread and cheese from a charcoal burner, in whose hovel he had passed the night. His royal father, being of an easygoing nature, believed the tale, but his mother was not so easily hoodwinked. She noticed that he now went hunting every day, and that he always had an excuse handy when he had slept two or three nights from home. She felt certain, therefore, that he had some love affair.

Two whole years passed since the marriage of the prince and princess, and during that time they had two children. The first, a daughter, was called "Dawn," while the second, a boy, was named "Day," because he seemed even more beautiful than his sister.

Many a time the queen told her son that he ought to settle down in life. She tried in this way to make him confide in her, but he did not dare to trust her with his secret. Despite the affection which he bore her, he was afraid of his mother, for she came of a race of ogres, and the king had only married her for her wealth.

It was whispered at the Court that she had ogreish instincts, and that when little children were near her she had the greatest difficulty in the world to keep herself from pouncing on them.

No wonder the prince was reluctant to say a word.

But at the end of two years the king died, and the prince found himself on the throne. He then made public announcement of his marriage, and went in state to fetch his royal consort from her castle. With her two children beside her she made a triumphal entry into the capital of her husband's realm.

Some time afterwards the king declared war on his neighbor, the Emperor Cantalabutte. He appointed the queen mother as regent in his absence, and entrusted his wife and children to her care.

He expected to be away at the war for the whole of the summer, and as soon as he was gone the queen mother sent her daughter-in-law and the two children to a country mansion in the forest. This she did that she might be able the more easily to gratify her horrible longings. A few days later she went there herself, and in the evening summoned the chief steward.

"For my dinner tomorrow," she told him, "I will eat little Dawn."

"Oh, Madam!" exclaimed the steward.

"That is my will," said the queen; and she spoke in the tones of an ogre who longs for raw meat.

"You will serve her with piquant sauce," she added.

The poor man, seeing plainly that it was useless to trifle with an ogress, took his big knife and went up to little Dawn's chamber. She was at that time four years old, and when she came running with a smile to greet him, flinging her arms round his neck and coaxing him to give her some sweets, he burst into tears, and let the knife fall from his hand.

Presently he went down to the yard behind the house, and slaughtered a young lamb. For this he made so delicious a sauce that his mistress declared she had never eaten anything so good.

At the same time the steward carried little Dawn to his wife, and bade the latter hide her in the quarters which they had below the yard.

Eight days later the wicked queen summoned her steward again.

"For my supper," she announced, "I will eat little Day."

The steward made no answer, being determined to trick her as he had done previously. He went in search of little Day, whom he found with a tiny foil in his hand, making brave passes-though he was but three years old-at a big monkey. He carried him off to his wife, who stowed him away in hiding with little Dawn. To the ogress the steward served up, in place of Day, a young kid so tender that she found it surpassingly delicious.

So far, so good. But there came an evening when this evil queen again addressed the steward.

"I have a mind," she said, "to eat the queen with the same sauce as you served with her children."

This time the poor steward despaired of being able to practice another deception. The young queen was twenty years old, without counting the hundred years she had been asleep. Her skin, though white and beautiful, had become a little tough, and what animal could he possibly find that would correspond to her? He made up his mind that if he would save his own life he must kill the queen, and went upstairs to her apartment determined to do the deed once and for all. Goading himself into a rage he drew his knife and entered the young queen's chamber. But a reluctance to give her no moment of grace made him repeat respectfully the command which he had received from the queen mother.

"Do it! do it!" she cried, baring her neck to him; "carry out the order you have been given! Then once more I shall see my children, my poor children that I loved so much!"

Nothing had been said to her when the children were stolen away, and she believed them to be dead.

The poor steward was overcome by compassion. "No, no, Madam," he declared; "you shall not die, but you shall certainly see your children again. That will be in my quarters, where I have hidden them. I shall make the queen eat a young hind in place of you, and thus trick her once more."

Without more ado he led her to his quarters, and leaving her there to embrace and weep over her children, proceeded to cook a hind with such art that the queen mother ate it for her supper with as much appetite as if it had indeed been the young queen.

The queen mother felt well satisfied with her cruel deeds, and planned to tell the king, on his return, that savage wolves had devoured his consort and his children. It was her habit, however, to prowl often about the courts and alleys of the mansion, in the hope of scenting raw meat, and one evening she heard the little boy Day crying in a basement cellar. The child was weeping because his mother had threatened to whip him for some naughtiness, and she heard at the same time the voice of Dawn begging forgiveness for her brother.

The ogress recognized the voices of the queen and her children, and was enraged to find she had been tricked. The next morning, in tones so affrighting that all trembled, she ordered a huge vat to be brought into the middle of the courtyard. This she filled with vipers and toads, with snakes and serpents of every kind, intending to cast into it the queen and her children, and the steward with his wife and serving girl. By her command these were brought forward, with their hands tied behind their backs.

There they were, and her minions were making ready to cast them into the vat, when into the courtyard rode the king! Nobody had expected him so soon, but he had traveled posthaste. Filled with amazement, he demanded to know what this horrible spectacle meant. None dared tell him, and at that moment the ogress, enraged at what confronted her, threw herself head foremost into the vat, and was devoured on the instant by the hideous creatures she had placed in it.

The king could not but be sorry, for after all she was his mother; but it was not long before he found ample consolation in his beautiful wife and children.

*The End.*

*Written by*
*Charles Perrault (1628-1703)*

*Translated by*
*A.E. Johnson (1921)*

# I.

# Pavane For The Sleeping Princess In The Woods

*(Pavane pour la Belle au Bois dormant)*

Maurice Ravel

# I.
# Pavane For The Sleeping Princess In The Woods

MAURICE RAVEL

Flt. 1
Flt. 2
Ob.
EH.
2 Cls.
Bsn.
FH.
Harp
Vlns. 1
Vlns. 2
Vlas.
Ces.
Bss. div.
Pno.
Solo
Muted pizz.
pizz.
m. g.
m. d.
1
7
8
9
10
11
12
13

Rall.
Flt. 1
Flt. 2
Ob.
EH.
2 Cls.
Bsn.
FH.
Harp
Muted
Vlns. 1
Vlns. 2
arco
Vlas.
arco
Ces.
div.
Bss. div.
Pno.
14
15
16
17
18
19
20

# PRACTICAL ANALYSIS

# PAVANE FOR THE SLEEPING PRINCESS IN THE WOODS

The original French title is *Pavane pour la Belle au Bois dormant*. While we have no notes on this movement, it appears that dramatically, Ravel is describing the scene in the castle after the princess and her household have been to sleep for a century in a spell cast by a fairy. The use of pizzicato suggests a last look as her mother and father, the King and Queen, walk through the castle and out the door. Ravel's use of the Aeolian mode suggests quiet sadness and resignation.

A Pavane is a slow and stately dance, here in a two-feel, Lento. As I look at the broad form, it's ABA, but a further breakdown shows $AA^1$ B $AA^1$ .

Having defined the form, let's look at the instrumentation.

## Orchestral Setup

We have:

Flute 1
Flute 2
Oboe
English Horn (Oboe 2)
Clarinet 1
Clarinet 2
French Horn 1
Harp
14 Violins 1 Muted
12 Violins 2 Muted
10 Violas Muted
8 Cellos Muted
6 Basses Muted

On your score, above the instrument names, write **14** over Vlns 1, **12** over Vlns 2, **10** over Violas, **8** over Cellos and **6** over Basses. Do it on each page.[1]

[1] If you're uncomfortable doing this on your score, do it on one of the optional PDF scores available for download from www.alexanderpublishing.com

This simple act will focus your thinking on orchestral balance and weighting. For example, while we have six Basses, they're divided. At bar 5, half the Basses are muted playing an harmonic while the other half are muted playing pizzicato.

## Melody and the 8 Keys of Professional Orchestration

| Bar Numbers | Instrument(s) | Which of the 8 Keys | Dynamics |
|---|---|---|---|
| 1 - 4 | Flute 2 | First Key | *pp* |
| 5 - 8 | Flute 1 | First Key | *pp* |
| 9 - 12 | Clarinet 1 | First Key | *p* |
| 13 - 17 | Flute 1 | First Key | *p* |
| 17 - 20 | Violins 1 | First Key | *pp* |

For this movement, we see the First Key, solo instruments or sections assigned to the melody. The melody starts in Flute 2 (bars 1 - 4) in the flute's middle register, then moves to Flute 1 in the flute's high register (bars 5 - 8). The Clarinet takes over the melody from the pick up to bar 9 through bar 13 (B). At the repeat of A, Flute 1 plays the first phrase. So to here, the melody moves by phrase from solo flute to solo clarinet, back to solo flute and finally at the second $A^1$, to the muted Violins 1.

At bars 17-20, we see the Fourth Key, the String section harmonized. Violins 1 are on the melody, while Violins 2 are on the counterline. The rest of the harmony is handled by a combination of muted strings playing a sustained pedal, with the Violas and 1/2 Basses filling in the harmony parts using harmonics. (See explanation below in $A^1$ Repeats).

### Dynamic Range

With the exception of bars 11 - 12 where the Cellos crescendo from a *p* to an *mf*, the entire piece ranges from *pp* ($AA^1$), to *p* (B), (A), to *pp* ($A^1$). So even the dynamics pretty much follow the form for this movement.

### Counterpoint Applied

As we look at *Mother Goose Suite*, be aware of Ravel's active use of counterpoint in each work. Bars 1 - 4 show a simple but deft use of what academically would be called "species" counterpoint. Then see bars 9-16 for practical three and four-part counterpoint mixed.

### Bars 1 - 4: *The First A and Orchestral Weighting*

Looking at the Piano part and then at the orchestral score, Ravel is orchestrating two lines. The melody line is performed by one instrument (Flute 2) while the counterline is played by 11 instruments.

Listening to the optional audio, although all the instruments are at *pp*, the solo Flute predominates while the muted Violas and muted French Horn sit back slightly in the mix.

What you should learn from this is that 10 muted Violas can play so quietly, and so delicately as to not overwhelm (or blow away) the solo Flute in the middle register.

Doubling the muted Violas is the muted French horn. Listen very carefully to the recording and notice how the muted French horn blends so well in the same register as the muted Violas. Listening closely, the muted French horn has a sort of mournful sound.

At bars 4 - 5, even though muted, note how just three basses project so clearly. At bar 5, the bass line is picked up by eight muted cellos sustaining.

## Bars 5 - 8: *The First $A^1$ and Orchestral Weighting*

Listen carefully to see how the mournful sound of the muted French horn moves to the Flute 2 in the same register.

**Jazz Cliché Line -** One note about the Flute 2 line. In jazz writing we call this an ascending cliché line. Often used in the blues, composer John Barry made this line famous with the James Bond Theme. But before 007, there was the blues. And Ravel, who frequented Paris' many jazz clubs absorbed this very common cliché line, made it his own, and incorporated it in this movement. In the first $A^1$ it's with the flute, in the second, it's with Violins 2.

In the Piano part you have an E pedal for four bars. Harmonically, we could look at bar 5 as being EMIN7b9, ESus4$^{ADD9}$, EMIN7(11), EMIN7$^{ADD9}$. Look at the bass harmonic in bar 5. Although the B (fifth of the chord) isn't in the Piano part, Ravel uses three basses to sound the B with harmonics. The "B" sounded is the B3 (third line B in the treble clef). We come up with this analysis because the moving cliché line changes the chord progressions and creates a dark (B9) to bright (9) coloration that you can hear and feel in Flute 2.

In bar 5 and continuing, you see D4 being repeated in quarter notes. In the score, the D is sustained and the motion is created by the cliché line.

So at A we have a very open sound. At $A^1$, Ravel creates a sustained "pad" using cellos (on the bass line sounding the root of the chord), bass harmonics sounding the fifth of the chord in the middle of the treble clef, a Bb clarinet doubling the root an octave above the cello, with the harp sounding the seventh.

## Bars 9 - 12: *B and Orchestral Weighting*

At B, we're back to a more open sound. Ravel passes the melody from the Flute to the Clarinet, but it's important to notice that the melody moves from the high register in the Flute to the high register of the Clarinet. In this register, the Clarinet can sound similar to the Flute. So this is a very subtle color change. As a contrasting color, Ravel selects the more somber English horn to play the counterline (see Piano part, treble clef beat two of bar 9). Initially the English horn is doubled by the muted Violins 1 playing pizzicato. Then beginning in bar 10, the bass part is broken down into two phrases, the first being played by the muted Violas, and the second by the muted Cellos, both playing pizzicato.

## Bars 13 - 16: *A Repeats Re-Orchestrated*

At bar 13 (see Piano part) we have a DMIN7 chord on beat 1. It's voiced: root, seventh, third, fifth (melody note). Now look at the Violas where Ravel has written a strummed quadruple stop. This is very subtle, but in the recording, it hints of sounding like a guitar.

Instead of doubling a muted solo French horn with the Violas, Ravel changes and doubles the English horn with the muted Violins 2 playing pizzicato.

Also at bar 13, the root (D) and the third (F) are sustained. This pad is created with Clarinet 2 playing the root and the French horn playing the third a tenth above. Motion comes from the English horn and the melody in the Flute.

## Bars 17 - 20: *$A^1$ Repeats Re-Orchestrated*

All of the strings are muted. The only instruments playing are the Harp and the strings. The melody passes from the solo Flute to the Violins 1. Basses and Cellos are divided.

**Lower Register** – Three basses bow the root of the chord (E). These Basses are doubled by the Harp (left hand) and the Cellos divided playing the E in octaves. So, a combination of Harp, seven basses and cellos are on the root, and five cellos on the root an octave above. So we have E in octaves in the lower register.

**High Register** – The melody is in the high register with Violins 1.

**Medium Register** – Look at the Piano part. D4, the seventh of the chord, is sounded by the Violas using harmonics and sustaining with the Harp doubling it. For motion, the Harp has the open D4 and then D4 created by harmonics. Notice that Ravel gives the Harpist time to setup the harmonic. One note on the Harp part. Within the recording, notice that you don't hear the harp at all on bars 5 - 8. I checked other recordings, and the same thing happens. In a live performance, this first part might be heard. But in various recordings, it's lost in the mix.

The B (fifth of the chord), though not written in the Piano part, is sounded from the harmonics of the bass part. The cliché line is performed by Violins 2.

**The Cliché Line** – When first used, the phrasing matches the Piano part. Now in its second use, instead of playing all four pitches under one bow, there are two pitches per bow.

**Bar 20** – The harmonic in the Bass sounds an A an octave and a fifth above. The violins are divided with seven players on a pitch in Violins 1 and six on a pitch in Violins 2.

To state the obvious, a lot of thinking went into this score.

## Stage Seating Position

Depending on how the orchestra is seated and mic'ed, you should hear the pizzicato in bars 9 - 12 moving across the stereo field as it travels from the violins on the left to the cellos on the right.

## Electronic Scoring Observation

What makes *Pavane* so colorful and intimate are muted strings, (including basses), string harmonics sounding from muted strings, and the muted French horn doubling the muted Violas.

Another scoring point is the divided strings, especially the divided basses, where half are either arco or pizzicato, and the other half are muted playing harmonics to fill in chord tones.

# Little Tom Thumb

## A Story by Charles Perrault

### *From "Contes du temps passé", (1697)*

Once upon a time there lived a woodcutter and his wife, who had seven children, all boys. The eldest was only ten years old, and the youngest was seven. People were astonished that the woodcutter had had so many children in so short a time, but the reason was that his wife delighted in children, and never had less than two at a time.

They were very poor, and their seven children were a great tax on them, for none of them was yet able to earn his own living. And they were troubled also because the youngest was very delicate and could not speak a word. They mistook for stupidity what was in reality a mark of good sense.

This youngest boy was very little. At his birth he was scarcely bigger than a man's thumb, and he was called in consequence "Little Tom Thumb." The poor child was the scapegoat of the family, and got the blame for everything. All the same, he was the sharpest and shrewdest of the brothers, if he spoke but little he listened much.

There came a very bad year, when the famine was so great that these poor people resolved to get rid of their family. One evening, after the children had gone to bed, the woodcutter was sitting in the chimney corner with his wife. His heart was heavy with sorrow as he said to her:

"It must be plain enough to you that we can no longer feed our children. I cannot see them die of hunger before my eyes, and I have made up my mind to take them tomorrow to the forest and lose them there. It will be easy enough to manage, for while they are amusing themselves by collecting fagots we have only to disappear without their seeing us."

"Ah!" cried the woodcutter's wife, "do you mean to say you are capable of letting your own children be lost?"

In vain did her husband remind her of their terrible poverty; she could not agree. She was poor, but she was their mother. In the end, however, reflecting what a grief it would be to see them die of hunger, she consented to the plan, and went weeping to bed.

Little Tom Thumb had heard all that was said. Having discovered, when in bed, that serious talk was going on, he had got up softly, and had slipped under his father's stool in order to listen without being seen. He went back to bed, but did not sleep a wink for the rest of the night, thinking over what he had better do. In the morning he rose very early and went to the edge of a brook. There he filled his pockets with little white pebbles and came quickly home again.

They all set out, and little Tom Thumb said not a word to his brothers of what he knew.

They went into a forest which was so dense that when only ten paces apart they could not see each other. The woodcutter set about his work, and the children began to collect twigs to make fagots. Presently the father and mother, seeing them busy at their task, edged gradually away, and then hurried off in haste along a little narrow footpath.

When the children found they were alone they began to cry and call out with all their might. Little Tom Thumb let them cry, being confident that they would get back home again. For on the way he had dropped the little white stones which he carried in his pocket all along the path.

"Don't be afraid, brothers," he said presently; "our parents have left us here, but I will take you home again. Just follow me."

They fell in behind him, and he led them straight to their house by the same path which they had taken to the forest. At first they dared not go in, but placed themselves against the door, where they could hear everything their father and mother were saying.

Now the woodcutter and his wife had no sooner reached home than the lord of the manor sent them a sum of ten crowns which had been owing from him for a long time, and of which they had given up hope. This put new life into them, for the poor creatures were dying of hunger.

The woodcutter sent his wife off to the butcher at once, and as it was such a long time since they had had anything to eat, she bought three times as much meat as a supper for two required.

When they found themselves once more at table, the woodcutter's wife began to lament.

"Alas! where are our poor children now?" she said; "they could make a good meal off what we have over. Mind you, William, it was you who wished to lose them: I declared over and over again that we should repent it. What are they doing now in that forest? Merciful heavens, perhaps the wolves have already eaten them! A monster you must be to lose your children in this way!"

At last the woodcutter lost patience, for she repeated more than twenty times that he would repent it, and that she had told him so. He threatened to beat her if she did not hold her tongue.

It was not that the woodcutter was less grieved than his wife, but she browbeat him, and he was of the same opinion as many other people, who like a woman to have the knack of saying the right thing, but not the trick of being always in the right.

"Alas!" cried the woodcutter's wife, bursting into tears, "where are now my children, my poor children?"

She said it once so loud that the children at the door heard it plainly. Together they all cried out:

"Here we are! Here we are!"

She rushed to open the door for them, and exclaimed, as she embraced them:

"How glad I am to see you again, dear children! You must be very tired and very hungry. And you, Peterkin, how muddy you are - come and let me wash you!"

This Peterkin was her eldest son. She loved him more than all the others because he was inclined to be redheaded, and she herself was rather red.

They sat down at the table and ate with an appetite which it did their parents good to see. They all talked at once, as they recounted the fears they had felt in the forest.

The good souls were delighted to have their children with them again, and the pleasure continued as long as the ten crowns lasted. But when the money was all spent they relapsed into their former sadness. They again resolved to lose the children, and to lead them much further away than they had done the first time, so as to do the job thoroughly. But though they were careful not to speak openly about it, their conversation did not escape little Tom Thumb, who made up his mind to get out of the situation as he had done on the former occasion.

But though he got up early to go and collect his little stones, he found the door of the house doubly locked, and he could not carry out his plan.

He could not think what to do until the woodcutter's wife gave them each a piece of bread for breakfast. Then it occurred to him to use the bread in place of the stones, by throwing crumbs along the path which they took, and he tucked it tight in his pocket.

Their parents led them into the thickest and darkest part of the forest, and as soon as they were there slipped away by a side path and left them. This did not much trouble little Tom Thumb, for he believed he could easily find the way back wherever he walked. But to his dismay he could not discover a single crumb. The birds had come along and eaten it all.

They were in sore trouble now, for with every step they strayed further, and became more and more entangled in the forest. Night came on and a terrific wind arose, which filled them with dreadful alarm. On every side they seemed to hear nothing but the howling of wolves which were coming to eat them up. They dared not speak or move.

In addition it began to rain so heavily that they were soaked to the skin. At every step they tripped and fell on the wet ground, getting up again covered with mud, not knowing what to do with their hands.

Little Tom Thumb climbed to the top of a tree, in an endeavor to see something. Looking all about him he espied, far away on the other side of the forest, a little light like that of a candle. He got down from the tree, and was terribly disappointed to find that when he was on the ground he could see nothing at all.

After they had walked some distance in the direction of the light, however, he caught a glimpse of it again as they were nearing the edge of the forest. At last they reached the house where the light was burning, but not without much anxiety, for every time they had to go down into a hollow they lost sight of it.

They knocked at the door, and a good dame opened to them. She asked them what they wanted.

Little Tom Thumb explained that they were poor children who had lost their way in the forest, and begged her, for pity's sake, to give them a night's lodging.

Noticing what bonny children they all were, the woman began to cry.

"Alas, my poor little dears!" she said; "you do not know the place you have come to! Have you not heard that this is the house of an ogre who eats little children?"

"Alas, madam!" answered little Tom Thumb, trembling like all the rest of his brothers, "what shall we do? One thing is very certain: if you do not take us in, the wolves of the forest will devour us this very night, and that being so we should prefer to be eaten by your husband. Perhaps he may take pity on us, if you will plead for us."

The ogre's wife, thinking she might be able to hide them from her husband till the next morning, allowed them to come in, and put them to warm near a huge fire, where a whole sheep was cooking on the spit for the ogre's supper.

Just as they were beginning to get warm they heard two or three great bangs at the door. The ogre had returned. His wife hid them quickly under the bed and ran to open the door.

The first thing the ogre did was to ask whether supper was ready and the wine opened. Then without ado he sat down to table. Blood was still dripping from the sheep, but it seemed all the better to him for that. He sniffed to right and left, declaring that he could smell fresh flesh.

"Indeed!" said his wife. "It must be the calf which I have just dressed that you smell."

"I smell fresh flesh, I tell you," shouted the ogre, eying his wife askance; "and there is something going on here which I do not understand."

With these words he got up from the table and went straight to the bed.

"Aha !" said he; "so this is the way you deceive me, wicked woman that you are! I have a very great mind to eat you too! It's lucky for you that you are old and tough! I am expecting three ogre friends of mine to pay me a visit in the next few days, and here is a tasty dish which will just come in nicely for them!"

One after another he dragged the children out from under the bed.

The poor things threw themselves on their knees, imploring mercy; but they had to deal with the most cruel of all ogres. Far from pitying them, he was already devouring them with his eyes, and repeating to his wife that when cooked with a good sauce they would make most dainty morsels.

Off he went to get a large knife, which he sharpened, as he drew near the poor children, on a long stone in his left hand.

He had already seized one of them when his wife called out to him. "What do you want to do it now for?" she said; "will it not be time enough tomorrow?"

"Hold your tongue," replied the ogre; "they will be all the more tender."

"But you have such a lot of meat," rejoined his wife; "look, there are a calf, two sheep, and half a pig."

"You are right," said the ogre; "give them a good supper to fatten them up, and take them to bed."

The good woman was overjoyed and brought them a splendid supper; but the poor little wretches were so cowed with fright that they could not eat.

As for the ogre, he went back to his drinking, very pleased to have such good entertainment for his friends. He drank a dozen cups more than usual, and was obliged to go off to bed early, for the wine had gone somewhat to his head.

Now the ogre had seven daughters who as yet were only children. These little ogresses all had the most lovely complexions, for, like their father, they ate fresh meat. But they had little round gray eyes, crooked noses, and very large mouths, with long and exceedingly sharp teeth, set far apart. They were not so very wicked at present, but they showed great promise, for already they were in the habit of killing little children to suck their blood.

They had gone to bed early, and were all seven in a great bed, each with a crown of gold upon her head.

In the same room there was another bed, equally large. Into this the ogre's wife put the seven little boys, and then went to sleep herself beside her husband.

Little Tom Thumb was fearful lest the ogre should suddenly regret that he had not cut the throats of himself and his brothers the evening before. Having noticed that the ogre's daughters all had golden crowns upon their heads, he got up in the middle of the night and softly placed his own cap and those of his brothers on their heads. Before doing so, he carefully removed the crowns of gold, putting them on his own and his brothers' heads. In this way, if the ogre were to feel like slaughtering them that night he would mistake the girls for the boys, and vice versa.

Things fell out just as he had anticipated. The ogre, waking up at midnight, regretted that he had postponed till the morrow what he could have done overnight. Jumping briskly out of bed, he seized his knife, crying: "Now then, let's see how the little rascals are; we won't make the same mistake twice!"

He groped his way up to his daughters' room, and approached the bed in which were the seven little boys. All were sleeping, with the exception of little Tom Thumb, who was numb with fear when he felt the ogre's hand, as it touched the head of each brother in turn, reach his own.

"Upon my word," said the ogre, as he felt the golden crowns; "a nice job I was going to make of it! It is very evident that I drank a little too much last night!"

Forthwith he went to the bed where his daughters were, and here he felt the little boys' caps.

"Aha, here are the little scamps!" he cried; "now for a smart bit of work!"

With these words, and without a moment's hesitation, he cut the throats of his seven daughters, and well satisfied with his work went back to bed beside his wife.

No sooner did little Tom Thumb hear him snoring than he woke up his brothers, bidding them dress quickly and follow him. They crept quietly down to the garden, and jumped from the wall. All through the night they ran in haste and terror, without the least idea of where they were going.

When the ogre woke up he said to his wife:

"Go upstairs and dress those little rascals who were here last night."

The ogre's wife was astonished at her husband's kindness, never doubting that he meant her to go and put on their clothes. She went upstairs, and was horrified to discover her seven daughters bathed in blood, with their throats cut.

She fell at once into a swoon, which is the way of most women in similar circumstances.

The ogre, thinking his wife was very long in carrying out his orders, went up to help her, and was no less astounded than his wife at the terrible spectacle which confronted him.

"What's this I have done?" he exclaimed. "I will be revenged on the wretches, and quickly, too!"

He threw a jugful of water over his wife's face, and having brought her round ordered her to fetch his seven-league boots, so that he might overtake the children.

He set off over the countryside, and strode far and wide until he came to the road along which the poor children were traveling. They were not more than a few yards from their home when they saw the ogre striding from hilltop to hilltop, and stepping over rivers as though they were merely tiny streams.

Little Tom Thumb espied near at hand a cave in some rocks. In this he hid his brothers, and himself followed them in, while continuing to keep a watchful eye upon the movements of the ogre.

Now the ogre was feeling very tired after so much fruitless marching (for seven-league boots are very fatiguing to their wearer), and felt like taking a little rest. As it happened, he went and sat down on the very rock beneath which the little boys were hiding. Overcome with weariness, he had not sat there long before he fell asleep and began to snore so terribly that the poor children were as frightened as when he had held his great knife to their throats.

Little Tom Thumb was not so alarmed. He told his brothers to flee at once to their home while the ogre was still sleeping soundly, and not to worry about him. They took his advice and ran quickly home.

Little Tom Thumb now approached the ogre and gently pulled off his boots, which he at once donned himself. The boots were very heavy and very large, but being enchanted boots they had the faculty of growing larger or smaller according to the leg they had to suit. Consequently they always fitted as though they had been made for the wearer.

He went straight to the ogre's house, where he found the ogre's wife weeping over her murdered daughters.

"Your husband," said little Tom Thumb, "is in great danger, for he has been captured by a gang of thieves, and the latter have sworn to kill him if he does not hand over all his gold and silver. Just as they had the dagger at his throat, he caught sight of me and begged me to come to you and thus rescue him from his terrible plight. You are to give me everything of value which he possesses, without keeping back a thing, otherwise he will be slain without mercy. As the matter is urgent he wished me to wear his seven-league boots, to save time, and also to prove to you that I am no impostor."

The ogre's wife, in great alarm, gave him immediately all that she had, for although this was an ogre who devoured little children, he was by no means a bad husband.

Little Tom Thumb, laden with all the ogre's wealth, forthwith repaired to his father's house, where he was received with great joy.

Many people do not agree about this last adventure, and pretend that little Tom Thumb never committed this theft from the ogre, and only took the seven-league boots, about which he had no compunction, since they were only used by the ogre for catching little children. These folks assert that they are in a position to know, having been guests at the woodcutter's cottage. They further say that when little Tom Thumb had put on the ogre's boots, he went off to the Court, where he knew there was great anxiety concerning the result of a battle which was being fought by an army two hundred leagues away.

They say that he went to the king and undertook, if desired, to bring news of the army before the day was out; and that the king promised him a large sum of money if he could carry out his project.

Little Tom Thumb brought news that very night, and this first errand having brought him into notice, he made as much money as he wished. For not only did the king pay him handsomely to carry orders to the army, but many ladies at the court gave him anything he asked to get them news of their lovers, and this was his greatest source of income. He was occasionally entrusted by wives with letters to their husbands, but they paid him so badly, and this branch of the business brought him in so little, that he did not even bother to reckon what he made from it.

After acting as courier for some time, and amassing great wealth thereby, little Tom Thumb returned to his father's house, and was there greeted with the greatest joy imaginable. He made all his family comfortable, buying newly created positions for his father and brothers. In this way he set them all up, not forgetting at the same time to look well after himself.

*The End.*

*Written by*
*Charles Perrault (1628-1703)*

*Translated by*
*A.E. Johnson (1921)*

# II.

# Little Tom Thumb

*(Petit Poucet)*

Maurice Ravel

# II.
# Little Tom Thumb

Ob.
Vlns. 1
Vlns. 2
Vlas.
Ces.
Bss.
Pno.
5
6
7
8
9
10
11

1
EH.
2 Cls.
Vlns. 1
Vlns. 2
Vlas.
Ces.
Bss.
Pno.
p espressivo
1°
p
mf
Muted
Muted
pizz.
3
12
13
14
15
16
17
18
19

2
1° Solo
2 Flts.
EH.
1° Solo
2 Cls.
Muted
2 FHs.
pp
Vlns. 1
Vlns. 2
Vlas.
Ces.
Bss.
Pno.
20
21
22
23
24
25
26

2 Flts.
Ob.
EH.
2 Cls.
2 FHs.
Vlns. 1
Vlns. 2
Vlas.
Ces.
Bss.
Pno.
3
mf
f molto espressivo
p
pp
arco
27
28
29
30
31
32
33
34

4 2° change to Piccolo
2 Flts.
Ob.
EH.
p espressivo
2 Cls.
pp
Vlns. 1
Vlns. 2
pp
Vlas.
pp
p
Ces.
p
Bss.
Pno.
p
35
36
37
38
39
40
41

EH.
2 Bsns.
1°
Vlns. 1
Vlns. 2
Vlas.
Ces.
pizz.
Bss.
Pno.
42
43
44
45
46
47
48
49

Picc.
Flt.
EH.
2 Cls.
2 Bsns.
2 FHs.
Vln. 1 Solo
Vln. 2 Solo
Vln. 3 Solo
Tutti
Vlns. 2
Vlas.
Ces.
Bss. div.
Pno.
5
1°
Solo
p espressivo
Unmuted
gliss
mf
on the fingerboard
Mute
arco
p prominent and expressive
50
51
52
53
54

6
7
Picc.
Flt.
Ob.
EH.
2 Cls.
2 Bsns.
2 FHs.
Vlns. 1
Vlns. 2
Vlas.
Cello Solo
Tutti
Bss. div.
Pno.
unis.
normal
remove mute
on the fingerboard
espressivo
55
56
57
58
59
60

Picc.
2 Bsns.
Vlns. 1 div.
Vlns. 2
Vlas.
Cello Solo
Tutti
Bss.
Pno.
Mute
Mute
Mute
p
8
61
62
63
64
65
66

8
Picc.
Solo
Flt.
pp
2 Bsns.
2 FHs.
pp
Vlns. 1
div.
Vlns. 2
Vlas.
p
pp
Ces.
div.
pp
pp
Bss.
pizz.
arco
pp
pp
pp
Pno.
m. d.
67
68
69
70
71
72
73

9
Poco rit.
Ob.
ppp
Vlns. 1
pp
Vlns. 2
Vlas. div.
4 Violas only
Ces.
Bss.
Pno.
74
75
76
77
78
79

# Practical Analysis

## Little Tom Thumb

## "Lost in the Woods"

Here's the story. Having run out of money to support their children for a second time, Tom Thumb's parents have taken he and his brothers and sisters deep into the woods, with the intention of abandoning them. This particular piece could easily be a film cue because of the thematic layout and length. This particular scene describes the birds eating the bread crumbs that Tom had thrown down to guide them back out of the woods.

### Orchestral Setup

For *Tom Thumb,* Ravel expands the orchestra to include:

Flute 1
Flute 2 (with Piccolo)
Oboe 1
English horn
2 Bb Clarinets
2 Bassoons
2 French Horns
14 Violins 1
12 Violins 2
10 Violas
8 Cellos
6 Basses

Mark the number of strings on each page as before. The key is Eb. Since this is a transposed score, the Bb Clarinets are in F and the French horns are in Bb.

### Form

There are three main themes. Theme A I'm calling *Apprehension* (my name, not Ravel's). Theme B I'm calling *Consoling*. Theme C I'm calling *Out of the Woods*.

Underneath the themes is a poignant background line in eighth-notes.

| | |
|---|---|
| **Bar 1 - 4** | Intro |
| **Bars 5 - 11** | Apprehension (A) |
| **Bars 12 - 22** | Consoling (B) |
| **Bars 23 - 26** | A[1] Transition |
| **Bars 27 - 39** | Development (expressing fear) |
| **Bars 40 - 50** | Consoling (B[1]) |
| **Bars 51 - 54** | The Woods at Night |
| **Bars 56 - 59** | Development (repeated) |
| **Bars 60 - 66** | Apprehension (A[1]) |
| **Bars 67 - 74** | Out of the Woods (C) |
| **Bars 75 - 79** | Intro |

Bars 1 - 4 are the under theme. Pick-ups to bar 5 leads us to *Fear*. Theme B, *Consoling*, begins at bar 12. A transition begins at 23 where Theme A, *Apprehension*, is restated building to a high at 33 - 34, subsiding, and leading back to a restatement of *Consoling*, this time in a new key. At bar 51, Ravel begins *The Woods at Night* where, with glissandi, trills and other orchestral effects the children begin hearing the sound of birds and other wild animals. Emotion rises and subsides into the first theme, *Apprehension*, which is now restated at bar 60. At bar 67 we hear Theme C, *Out of The Woods*, with its lilting walking feel, which then weaves back to the *Apprehension* motive.

## Melody and the 8 Keys of Professional Orchestration

Applying the 8 Keys, we see that Ravel assigns the melody to a solo instrument and moves it to other solo instruments, often within the woodwind section. Below, the + sign means *unison* while the – sign means *octaves*

| Bar Numbers | Instrument(s) | Which of the 8 Keys | Dynamics |
|---|---|---|---|
| 1 - 4 | Vlns 1 – Vlns 2 | Second Key | *pp* |
| 5 - 11 | Oboe | First Key | *pp* |
| 12 - 22 | English Horn | First Key | *p* |
| 23 - 24 | Clarinet | First Key | *pp* |
| 25 - 26 | Flute 1 | First Key | *pp* |
| 27 - 31 | String Section | Third Key | *pp to f* |
| 32 - 39 | Orchestra | Fifth Key | *mf to pp* |
| 40 - 50 | English Horn | First Key | *p to mf*<br>*mf to p* |
| 51 - 54 | Violas & Bassoons | Third Key | *p* |
| 55 - 59 | Orchestra | Fifth Key | *pp to mf*<br>*mf to pp* |
| 60 - 66 | Piccolo | First Key | *pp* |
| 67 - 74 | Flute 2 | First Key | *pp* |
| 75 - 79 | Vlns 1 & Vlns 2 plus Oboe | Second Key | *pp* |

## Dynamic Range

The piece is largely *pp* and *p* until bar 27 where an extended crescendo begins and then quiets down back at bar 40 to *p*. *The Woods At Night*, beginning at 51, employs a mixture of dynamics to create the backdrop, then comes back down to *pp* and stays there until the end.

## Bars 1 - 4

Muted Violins, not divided, set up the mood. From bars 1 - 4, the under theme is in Violins 1 and the harmony in Violins 2. Compare the bowing to the Piano parts phrasing. It should not be assumed that Ravel has merely written the violins in thirds. Since there's a clear melodic theme present, we can look at this as two-part counterpoint note-against-note where the harmony is implied. This changes in bar 4 where the Oboe enters. One might ask, "Is this three-part counterpoint or is the melody simply harmonized in triads with the Oboe on the melody and the violins playing the supporting harmony?"

## Bars 5 - 11: *Apprehension*

As with a chorale or a jazz sectional, the melody is voiced down and harmonized in triads. You could also look at this as an application of the Fifth Key.

## Bars 12 - 22: *Consoling*

Besides the new *Consoling* theme, Ravel changes color by having the English horn play the theme supported underneath by muted violas and cellos. The splash of color to create a fourth part occurs in bars 14 and 17 (see Piano part) with a single Bb Clarinet playing the low E doubled by pizzicato bass.

## Bars 23 - 39: *Apprehension Restated and Builds*

The *Apprehension* motive is first restated in the clarinet then moves to the flute. At bar 27 emotions build. From bars 27 - 32 we have a masterful use of practical four-part counterpoint. Ravel has a sustaining pitch in the bass. The first and third parts are in 6ths and the second part is syncopated. Listen carefully to the effect it creates.

To set the feel, Ravel starts with the string section only: Violins 2, Violas, Cellos and Basses. Working up harmonically, Basses on the bottom G, Cellos and Violins 2 are in 6ths, Violas play the syncopated line.

At bar 30, the Basses drop out and we now have Violins 1, Violins 2, Violas and Cellos. The syncopation in the Violas is now passed off to Violins 2.

At bar 32, we now see at a dynamic range of *mf* to *f*, Ravel doubling instruments together. In the woodwinds, bar 33, Flute 1 + Oboe 1 – Flute 2 + English horn.

Clarinets catch the inner harmony parts. Look and see that the Violins 1 and Cellos are in octaves with the inner harmonies handled by Violins 2 and the Violas.

**Dramatic Scoring Note –** As tension and emotion rise and the orchestra is rising melodically to match the feel, consider leaving out the Basses since the basses provide an anchor.

## Bars 40 - 50: *Consoling*

Ravel is back to three parts, key change, English horn in lead over the muted Violas and Cellos.

## Bars 51 - 54: *The Woods At Night*

These four bars are genius in orchestration. Look at the bass clef in the Piano part. Here there's a line harmonized in sixths then in other intervals over the next few bars. This is a variant of *Apprehension*. The melody (upper voice) is assigned to a single Bassoon and the counterline to the Violas. The sustained D is assigned to the Basses.

Ravel divides Violins 1 so that there are three violin soloists. All three are unmuted. The birdsong in 51 and 53 is assigned to Violin 1 solo and is created using harmonics and glisses. In the solo Violin 2 and 3 in bars 52 and 54, also unmuted, trills create the sensation of a breeze.

Additional birdsong is handled by the Piccolo and Flute 2 in 52 and 54.

## Bars 55 - 59: *The Woods At Night*

Ravel is back to four-part counterpoint in 55-59 using imitation to continue restating the *Apprehension* motive. As Ravel builds to another crescendo, this time the string section is anchored with the Basses.

## Bars 60 - 66: *Apprehension*

The theme is placed with the Piccolo doubled two octaves below by a solo Cello. Violins 2 and Violas carry the moving harmony in this section above the solo Cello line. Again, another practical usage of counterpoint.

## Bars 67 - 74: *Out of the Woods*

The music represents a sigh of relief as the children clear the woods. The melody has a lilting walking quality to it supported by pizzicato in the Basses. The chromatic line in the Violas is similar to the cliché line found in *Pavane*. Look at the sustained half notes in the Piano part at 67. Ravel lowers the top E by an octave, then assigns the sustained thirds to the French horns.

## Bars 75 - 79: Apprehension

We have a restatement of the opening with Violins 1 and 2 muted and in thirds. The Oboe enters at 78 to restate the motive. It closes with Ravel creating the sustaining harmony from harmonics in the divided Cellos.

## Electronic Scoring Considerations

1. Check the range of the English horn to make certain it can execute this passage.

2. Muted strings - many libraries claim muted strings, but you must check to see if they were *recorded* muted, or recorded open and *programmed* to sound muted.

3. Very few "muted" string libraries at this writing can execute bars 1 - 30. Check to make sure that there are articulations available to execute this passage.

# Green Serpent

## A Story by Madame D'Aulnoy

### *From "Contes Nouveaux ou Les Fées à la Mode"*, (1698)

Once upon a time there was a great queen who gave birth to twin daughters. She invited twelve fairies who lived in the neighbourhood to come and see them, and bestow gifts on them according to the custom of the time. And a very convenient custom it was! For the fairies' power very often remedied what Nature had done ill, although occasionally it spoiled what Nature had done very well.

When the fairies were all in the banqueting hall, a magnificent repast was served. Just as they were sitting down to table, Magotine entered. She was the sister of Carabosse, and was equally wicked. The queen trembled at the sight, fearing some disaster, for she had not invited her to the feast; but carefully concealing her anxiety, she went to find for Magotine a green velvet armchair embroidered with sapphires. As Magotine was the oldest of the fairies, they all moved to make room for her, and each whispered the other:

"Let us hasten to bestow our gifts on the little princess, in order to anticipate Magotine."

On the offer of the armchair, Magotine said rudely that she did not want it; she was tall enough to eat standing. But she made a great mistake, for, as the table was rather high, she could not even see it, so small was she! This vexed her so greatly that her ill-temper increased.

"Madam," said the queen, "I beg you to sit down to table."

"If you had wanted me," said the fairy, "you would have invited me with the rest; you only ask handsome people with fine figures and magnificently attired like my sisters to your court; as for me, I'm too old and ugly. But, all the same, my power is as great as theirs, and without boasting at all, even greater."

The fairies urged her so much to sit down to table that she at last consented. A golden basket was placed on it, containing a dozen packets of precious stones; the first-comers helped themselves, and there were thus none left for Magotine, who began to mutter below her breath. The queen went to her closet, and brought her a casket of perfumed Spanish leather, covered with rubies and filled with diamonds; she entreated Magotine to accept it, but the fairy shook her head, saying:

"Keep your jewels, I have enough and to spare. I only came to see if you had remembered me, and you had entirely forgotten my existence."

So saying, she struck her wand on the table, and all the good things upon it immediately turned into fricasseed serpents. The fairies, in great alarm, threw down their serviettes, and left the banqueting hall.

While they were discussing the evil trick Magotine had just played them, the cruel little fairy approached the cradle where the princesses lay wrapped in the prettiest cloth of gold swaddling clothes imaginable.

"My gift to you," she said quickly to one, "is that you shall be the ugliest creature in the world."

She was on the point of laying a like curse on the other when the fairies ran up in great agitation and prevented her. Wicked Magotine broke a window-pane, and passing through it like a flash of lightning, disappeared from view.

No matter what gifts the good fairies bestowed on the princess, the queen was less sensible of their kindness than of the pain of finding herself mother of the ugliest creature in the world. She took her in her arms, and was grieved to see her grow uglier from one minute to the next. She tried in vain to keep from crying in the presence of the fairies, but she could not control herself, and they showed her all the pity imaginable.

"What shall we do," they consulted, "to console the queen?"

They held a great council, and afterwards told her not to grieve so deeply, since, at an appointed time, her daughter would be very happy.

"But," interrupted the queen, "will she become beautiful?"

"We cannot," they replied, "explain ourselves more fully: let it suffice you that your daughter will be happy."

She thanked them, and did not fail to load them with presents, for, although the fairies are very rich, they always like to receive gifts. The custom has since passed to all the peoples of the earth, and time has not destroyed it.

The queen called her elder daughter Laidronette, and the younger Bellotte. The names suited them admirably; for Laidronette became so ugly, that in spite of her great intelligence, it was impossible to look at her; her sister grew very beautiful and was most charming. When Laidronette was twelve years old, she threw herself at the feet of the king and queen, and begged their permission to shut herself up in the castle of solitude, in order to hide her ugliness, and not grieve them any longer. They loved her, her ugliness notwithstanding, and it cost them something to consent, but there was Bellotte, and that sufficed to console them.

Laidronette asked the queen to send with her only her nurse and a few officers.

"You needn't fear that any one will run away with me, and for myself, I confess, fashioned as I am, I should like to avoid even the light of day."

The king and queen granted her request, and she was conveyed to the castle of her choice. It had been built many centuries before. The sea came right up to the windows, and did duty for an ornamental canal. A vast forest near at hand furnished pleasant walks, and meadows shut in the view. The princess played musical instruments, and sang divinely. She spent two years in that pleasant solitude, and wrote several books of reflections, but the desire of seeing her parents again made her get into her coach and go to the court.

She arrived exactly on Bellotte's wedding day. Everybody was filled with joy, but at the sight of Laidronette they all looked annoyed. Neither the king nor queen embraced or caressed her, and for all welcome they told her she had grown much uglier, and advised her not to appear at the ball; if however she wished to see it, some place might be arranged whence she could view it.

She replied that she had not come to dance, nor to listen to the music, but she had been so long in the lonely castle that she could not help leaving it to pay her duty to the king and queen. She knew, to her keen regret, that they could not endure her, and she intended returning to her solitude, where the trees, flowers and springs did not reproach her for her ugliness every time she went near them. The king and queen, observing her sorrow, told her she could remain with them two or three days. But having a heart, Laidronette replied that if she spent that time in such pleasant company, it would pain her too much to leave them. They were too anxious for her to go to seek to prevent her, and coldly told her she was right.

Princess Bellotte gave her for a wedding gift an old riband she had worn all the winter on her muff, and the king she was marrying presented her with some purple silk for a petticoat. Had she consulted her own feelings, she would have thrown the riband and silk in the faces of the generous donors who treated her so ill; but she had too much spirit, wisdom and intelligence to show her annoyance, and set out with her faithful nurse on her return to the castle. So full of sorrow was her heart that during the whole journey she did not open her lips.

Walking one day in the thickest part of the forest, she saw under a tree a big green serpent. Raising his head, he said:

"Laidronette, you are not alone in misfortune. Look at my horrible form, and learn that I was born even more beautiful than you."

The princess, greatly alarmed, heard only half of what he said, and for several days, fearing such another encounter, dared not stir out. At length, weary of always being alone in her room, she one evening quitted it, and went to walk by the sea-shore. She was pacing slowly along, thinking over her sad fate, when she saw a little gilded boat, painted with a thousand different devices, come towards her. The sail was of brocade of gold, the mast of cedarwood, and the oars of calambac. Chance alone seemed its steersman, and as it stopped close to the shore, the princess, curious to see its beauties, stepped in.

She found it adorned with crimson velvet with a gold ground, the nails being made of diamonds. But all of a sudden the boat left the shore, and the princess, alarmed at her danger, took the oars to try and return, but all her efforts were of no avail. The wind raised the waves up mountains high, she lost sight of land, and seeing nothing but sea and sky, abandoned herself to her fate, sure that the worst was about to happen, and that she owed this bad turn to Magotine.

"I must perish," she cried; "but what secret impulse makes me fear death? Alas! So far, I have known none of the pleasures that could make me hate it. My ugliness alarms even my nearest relatives; my sister is a great queen, while I am banished to the depths of a desert, where all the society I have found is a talking serpent. Would not death be preferable to a wearisome existence like this?"

These reflections dried the princess's tears. She looked boldly to see from what quarter death would come, and seemed to be inviting it not to delay, when she saw a serpent on the waves approaching the boat. He said:

"If you are willing to receive help from a poor green serpent like me, I can save your life."

"Death strikes less terror to my heart than you do," exclaimed the princess; "and if you want to do me a favour, never show yourself in my sight." Green Serpent made a long hissing sound, which he meant for a sigh, and answering never a word, plunged into the sea.

"What a horrid monster!" said the princess to herself; "he has green wings, a many-colored body, ivory jaws, fiery eyes, and long, bristling hair. Ah! I would rather die than owe my life to him. But," she went on, "what makes him follow me so persistently? And how comes it that he speaks like a reasoning being?"

She was considering thus when a voice replying to her thought said:

"Learn, Laidronette, that Green Serpent is not to be despised; and were it not too cruel a thing to say, I could assure you that he is less ugly in his degree than you are in yours. But so far from wishing to anger you, if you would only consent, I should like to mitigate your sorrow."

The voice vastly surprised the princess, and what it said was so little credible, that she had not strength enough to keep back her tears. But suddenly reflecting:

"What!" she cried; "reproached with my ugliness as I am, I will not lament my death. What is the use of being the most beautiful woman in the world? I must die all the same. It ought rather to console me and prevent me regretting my life."

While she moralized, the boat drifting at the mercy of the waves struck a rock, and scarcely two pieces of the wood held together. The poor princess found her philosophy of no avail in so pressing a danger; she discovered a few pieces of wood, and imagining she was clinging to them she felt herself lifted up, and reached in safety the foot of a big rock. Alas! what were her sensations on finding she was tightly embracing Green Serpent! Seeing her great alarm he moved a little aside, and cried out:

"If you knew me better you would fear me less, but it is my cruel fate to terrify everybody."

He immediately threw himself into the water, and Laidronette was left alone on the great rock.

Casting her eyes around, she saw nothing to lessen her despair. Night was coming on; she had nothing to eat, and knew not where to find shelter.

"I thought," she said, sadly, "to end my days in the sea. Doubtless the last scene of all is to be here; some sea monster will devour me, or I shall perish of hunger."

She seated herself on the top of the rock. As long as the light lasted she looked out over the sea, and when night was over all the earth she took off her silk petticoat, covered her head and face with it, and anxiously awaited what might happen.

At length she fell asleep ; and it seemed to her that she heard a sound as of various musical instruments. She felt convinced she was dreaming, but after a moment she heard these lines sung, lines which seemed composed for her:

*Here within this palace gay*
*May you suffer Cupid's dart!*
*Here shall gladness be our part,*
*Sorrows all he'll drive away.*
*Here within this palace gay*
*May you suffer Cupid's dart!"*

The attention with which she listened to these words completely roused her.

"What happiness and what ill-fortune are in store for me?" she said. "In my condition, can happy days be possible for me?"

In terror, she opened her eyes, fearing to see herself surrounded by monsters. But imagine her astonishment, when, instead of the horrible and barren rock, she found herself in a chamber all panelled with gold. The bed on which she was reclining was in keeping with the splendor of the most beautiful palace in the world; she asked herself question after question, unable to believe she was actually awake. At last she got up and opened a glass door that led on to a spacious balcony, whence she descried all the beauty that Nature, seconded by art, could produce: gardens full of flowers, fountains, statues and rare trees; forests in the distance; palaces whose walls were adorned with precious stones and roofs of pearl, and so marvelously were they wrought that each was a masterpiece. The sea, calm and peaceful, was covered with numerous ships of all sorts, and the sails, streamers, and pennants tossing in the wind, produced the most charming possible effect.

"Oh, ye gods! ye just gods!" she exclaimed, "what do I see? Where am I? What a remarkable change! What has become of the terrible rock that seemed to threaten the heavens with its cloud-capped points? Was it I who nearly perished yesterday, and was saved by the aid of a serpent?"

In her distress she broke out into laments, now walking to and fro, now stopping still. At length she heard a noise in the room. Turning back into it, she saw coming towards her a hundred pagodas, adorned and built in a hundred different ways. The biggest were about an arm's length in height, and the smallest not more than four fingers; some beautiful, graceful, and pleasant looking; others hideous, and of a terrible ugliness. They were of diamonds, emeralds, rubies, pearls, crystal, amber, coral, porcelain, gold, silver, brass, bronze, iron, wood, clay; some without arms, others without feet, with mouths reaching from ear to ear, squint eyes, flat noses. In short, there is not greater unlikeness between the creatures who inhabit the world than there was between those pagodas.

Those who presented themselves before the princess were the deputies of the kingdom. After making her a speech containing many wise reflections they told her, to amuse her, that they had for some time been travelling about the world, but that in order to obtain their sovereign's consent they swore in setting out never to speak; and so scrupulous had they been that they would not move either head, feet, or hands. The greater number, however, could not help doing so, while they were thus travelling about the world. When they returned, they delighted their king by the recital of all the most secret affairs of the different courts in which they had been received.

"It is, madam," added the deputies, "a pleasure we will sometimes give you, for we are commanded to omit nothing in our power to amuse you. Instead of bringing you presents, we shall divert you with our songs and dances."

They immediately began to sing these words, dancing a round dance with tambourines and castanets:

*"Joy is more delightful*
*That follows after pain;*

*Joy is more delightful*
*After ills despiteful:*
*Young lovers, do not break your chain,*
*Let fortune you disdain,*
*Yet happiness you'll gain"*

When they had finished, the deputy who was spokesman said to the princess: "Here, madam, are a hundred pagodinas who are appointed to the honor of attending you: everything you most desire will be accomplished, provided you remain with us."

The pagodinas then appeared. They carried baskets in proportion to their size, filled with a hundred different things, so pretty, so useful, so well made, and so rich that Laidronette could not leave off admiring, praising and loudly expressing her wonder at the marvels she saw. The most distinguished of the pagodinas, a little diamond figure, suggested that as the heat was increasing, she should enter the bathing grotto. The princess walked in the direction pointed out, between two rows of body-guards of most laughable size and appearance. She found two basins of crystal ornamented with gold, and filled with choicely perfumed water, a canopy of cloth of gold was arranged over them. She asked why there were two basins, and was told that one was for her, and the other for the King of the Pagodas.

"But," she cried, "where is he?"

"Madam," was the reply, "he is just now at the wars; you will see him on his return."

The princess asked if he was married; she was told no, that he was so charming that so far he had not found any one worthy of him. She did not carry her curiosity further, she undressed and went into the bath. Immediately the pagodas and pagodinas began to sing and to play on musical instruments. Some had lutes made of a walnut-shell, others violas made of an almond-shell, for it was necessary to suit the instruments to their size. But everything was so exact and harmonised so well that nothing could be more delightful than these concerts.

When the princess came out of the bath, a magnificent dressing-gown was presented to her. Pagodas, playing the flute and the hautboy, walked before her; pagodinas followed her, singing songs in her honor. Thus she entered a room where her toilette was prepared. Immediately pagodinas who did duty as ladies of the bed-chamber and ladies' maids came and went, dressed her hair, attired her, praised her, applauded her. There was no longer any thought of ugliness, of purple silk petticoat, or of worn-out riband.

The princess was veritably astonished. "What," she said, "can procure me this extraordinary delight? I was on the point of perishing. I was awaiting death and could hope for nothing else, when suddenly I find myself in the most beautiful and magnificent place in the world, where my presence too seems to give so much pleasure!"

She possessed so much intelligence and goodness of heart, and her manners were so pleasing, that all the little creatures were charmed with her. Every day on rising new clothes, new laces, new jewels were brought her. It was certainly a great pity she was so ugly, but in consequence of the great care taken in dressing her, she who had never been able to endure the sight of herself, began to find herself less hideous.

The pagodas constantly told her the most secret and curious things that went on in the world. They told her of treaties of peace and leagues of war; of the treachery and quarrels of lovers, and the unfaithfulness of mistresses, of despairs, reconciliations, and disappointed heirs, of frustrated marriages and old widows who married again most unseasonably, of treasures discovered, of bankruptcies and fortunes made in a moment, of fallen favorites and besieged cities, of jealous husbands and flirting women, of thankless children and ruined towns. Indeed what did they not tell the princess to amuse and divert her? Some of the pagodas were most surprisingly swollen and puffed out. On asking the reason they told her:

"As we are not allowed when on our travels to laugh or to speak, and as we continually see very laughable things and the greatest absurdities, the effort not to laugh causes us to swell in this way. It is in fact a dropsy caused by suppressed laughter, of which we are cured when we return here."

The princess admired the good humor of the pagoda race, for people might indeed become inflated by constantly suppressing laughter at all the absurd things they must infallibly see.

Every evening one of the finest plays of Corneille or Moliisre was represented. Balls were of frequent occurrence. So that no possible effect might be lost, the tiniest figures danced on the tight-rope that they might be better seen, and the repasts served to the princess would have done for the banquets of some solemn festival. Books, serious, amusing, and historical, were brought to her; indeed the days passed like minutes. As a matter of fact, however, the pagodas, highly intelligent as they were, were of a ridiculous minuteness. It often happened when going a walk that she put thirty of them into her pocket to amuse her, and it was the pleasantest thing in the world to hear them chattering in their little voices, shriller than those of marionettes.

Once when the princess was unable to sleep, she said: "What will become of me? Shall I always remain here? My life passes more pleasantly than I could have dared to hope, yet my heart lacks something, and I cannot tell what it is. I begin to feel that a series of the same pleasures, varied by no events, is very insipid."

"Ah! princess," replied a voice, "is it not your own fault? If you would love, you would at once be conscious that it is quite possible to be happy for a very long time in a palace or even in a lonely desert with one we love."

"What pagoda is speaking to me?" she said. "What pernicious advice he gives me, opposed to all the peace of my life."

"It is no pagoda," came the reply, "that warns you of what must be sooner or later. It is the unhappy monarch of this kingdom who adores you, and only dares confess it in the greatest fear and trembling."

"A king adores me!" said the princess. "Has he eyes, or is he blind? Has he seen that I am the ugliest creature in the world?"

"I have seen you, madam," replied the invisible king, "and to me you are not what you represent yourself to be, and whether on account of your person, your merits, or your misfortunes, I can only repeat that I adore you, and that my timid and respectful love compels me to hide myself."

"I am deeply grateful to you," rejoined the princess. "Alas! what should I do if I loved any one?"

"You would make one happy who cannot live without you," he said, "and without your permission he would never dare to appear."

"No," said the princess, "I do not wish to see anything that might attract me."

Nothing further was said, but for the rest of the night she was greatly taken up with the circumstance.

Notwithstanding her resolution to say nothing about it, she could not help asking the pagodas if their king had returned. They replied: "No." That answer, which agreed ill with what she had heard, somewhat disturbed her, and she went on to ask if their king was young and good-looking. They told her he was young, handsome, and everything that was charming; she asked if they often heard from him, and they replied: "Every day."

"But does he know," she added, "that I am in his palace?"

"Yes" was the rejoinder, " he knows everything about you, and so great is his interest in you that couriers are sent from hour to hour to take him news of you."

She was silent, and began to reflect much more deeply than had been her custom.

When she was alone the voice spoke to her. At one time she was afraid of it; at another it gave her pleasure, for it invariably said the most gallant things.

"Notwithstanding my firm resolve never to love," said the princess, "and the good reason I have to keep out of my heart an emotion that can only cause me misery, I confess I should like to know a king whose taste is so eccentric as yours, for if you really do love me, you are probably the only person in the world who could care for a woman as ugly as I am."

"Think whatever you like of my taste, beloved princess," replied the voice, "I find justification enough in your merit; indeed it is not for that reason I am compelled to hide myself. The cause is so sad that if you knew it, you could not withhold your pity."

The princess then urged the voice to explain, but it spoke no more, and only long-drawn sighs were heard. She was greatly disturbed by all this; although her lover was invisible and unknown he was most attentive, and she was beginning to wish for more suitable society than that afforded by the pagodas. She was, in fact, getting very weary, and could only find pleasure in the voice of her invisible lover.

On one of the darkest nights in the year, awaking out of her sleep, she perceived some one close to her bed; she thought it was the pagodina of pearls, who, being much more intelligent than the others, sometimes came to talk with her. The princess stretched forth her arms to take hold of her; her hand was at once seized, pressed and kissed; she felt tears fall on it, and she was so startled that she could not speak. She had no doubt that it was the invisible king.

"What do you want of me?" she said, with a sigh. "Can I love you without knowing you, or seeing you?"

"Ah! madam," was the reply, "what are the conditions of pleasing you? It is impossible for me to show myself. The wicked Magotine, who played you such an evil trick, has condemned me to a penance of seven years; five have already gone, but two still remain, and if you were willing to take me for your husband, you could sweeten their bitterness. You think me very bold, and that what I ask of you is absolutely impossible; but if you knew the ardor of my passion, or the greatness of my misfortunes, you would not refuse the favour I beg of you."

As I have already said, Laidronette was becoming very weary; she found that, as far as intelligence went, he was all that could be desired, and under the specious name of a generous pity the invisible king won her heart and love. She replied that she required a few days in which to make up her mind. It was indeed a great thing to have brought matters so far, to a delay of a few days, for he had not dared to indulge hope. The fetes and concerts were redoubled, and only wedding hymns were sung before her, and presents, which surpassed anything she had ever seen, were continually brought her. The tender voice, ever assiduous, spoke love to her as soon as it was night, and the princess retired early, in order to have more time to converse with it.

At length she consented to marry the invisible king, and promised not to look upon him until his penance was at an end.

"Therein lies everything for you and me," he said. "If you give way to indiscreet curiosity, I should have to begin my penance all over again, and you would share the hardship with me: but if you can refrain from following the bad advice that will be given you, you will find that I shall be exactly to your taste, and you will at the same time recover the marvellous beauty taken from you by the wicked Magotine."

The princess, enchanted with that new hope, swore a thousand times to her husband to do nothing contrary to his wishes. The marriage was concluded without noise or splendor; but the heart and soul were not the less content.

As all the pagodas sought eagerly to amuse their new queen, one of them brought her the story of Psyche that a fashionable author had just written out in beautiful language; she found in it many things that bore upon her own adventure. She was seized with so violent a desire to receive her father and mother, her sister and brother-in-law, at the palace, that nothing the king could say could drive the fancy from her mind.

"The book you are reading," he added, "will teach you what were Psyche's misfortunes. I beg of you take heed and avoid them."

She promised even more than he asked, and a vessel of pagodas carrying presents and letters from Queen Laidronette to her mother was despatched. She implored her to pay her a visit in her kingdom, and for that occasion only the pagodas had permission to speak elsewhere than in their own country.

The loss of the princess had evoked a feeling of tenderness in her near relatives. They thought she was dead, and thus her letters were the more eagerly welcomed at the court. The queen, who was dying to see her daughter again, did not delay a moment in setting out with her daughter and son-in-law. The pagodas, who alone knew the road to their kingdom, acted as guides to the royal party, and when Laidronette saw her parents she thought she should die of joy. She read the story of Psyche over and over again as a safeguard against her replies to all the things her family said to her.

She had enough to do, and got into confusion a hundred times a day. Sometimes the king was with the army. Sometimes he was ill and so bad-tempered that he did not wish to see any one. Now he was on a pilgrimage, then he was hunting or fishing. It seemed she was fated to say nothing that carried any weight, and that cruel Magotine had bereft her of her good sense. Her mother and sister talked over the matter together, and came to the conclusion that Laidronette was deceiving them, and perhaps deceiving herself. With ill-judged zeal they determined to speak to her. They accomplished the task with so much skill that a thousand fears and doubts crept into Laidronette's mind. For a long time she had not permitted all they could say to have the least effect on her; but she now confessed that, so far, she had never seen her husband. His conversation, however, was so full of charm that to be happy it was only necessary to hear him. She told them further that his penance was to last two years more, and at the end of that period not only would she see him, but she would become as beautiful as the day-star. '

"Ah! wretched girl," exclaimed the queen, "how clear is the snare laid for you! Is it possible you can be simple enough to believe such tales? Your husband is a monster: it cannot be otherwise, for all the pagodas over whom he rules are the most grotesque creatures possible."

"I rather believe," replied Laidronette, "that he is the God of Love himself."

"What a mistaken notion!" exclaimed Queen Bellotte; "Psyche was told she had a monster for a husband, and found him to be Cupid himself. You persist in believing your husband is Love and assuredly you will discover him to be a monster. Any way set your mind at ease, enlighten yourself on so simple a matter." The queen was of the same opinion, and her son-in-law even more strongly so.

The poor princess was so confused and disturbed that, after sending away her family with presents that more than made up for the purple silk and the muff riband, she determined, happen what might, to see her husband. Ah! Fatal curiosity. A thousand terrible examples cannot cure us, and dearly indeed did the unfortunate princess pay for her indiscretion. She would have been very sorry not to follow the example of her predecessor, Psyche, so she concealed a lamp and with its aid looked upon the invisible king, so dear to her heart. But how terrible were her shrieks, when, instead of Love, gentle, fair, young, and altogether charming, she saw hideous Green Serpent with his long bristling hair. He awoke, transported with rage and despair:

"Oh! cruel one!" he cried, "is this the reward of my great love?" The princess heard no more, she swooned with fear, and Serpent was already far away.

Hearing the noise caused by this tragedy, some of the pagodas rushed in. They put the princess to bed, and assisted to restore her. When she came to herself, her condition may be more easily imagined than described. How she reproached herself for the evil she had brought upon her husband! She loved him tenderly, but abhorred his form, and would have given half her life never to have seen him.

The entrance of several pagodas with terrified countenances interrupted her sad reflections. They informed her that a number of ships full of marionettes, with Magotine at their head, had entered the harbor unopposed. The marionettes and pagodas are eternal enemies, and are rivals in a thousand things. The marionettes have even the privilege of speaking wherever they like, a thing the pagodas are denied. Magotine was their queen. Her hatred for poor Green Serpent and unfortunate Laidronette led her to assemble troops, and determine to attack them just when their sorrows should be at their height.

It was not difficult to succeed in her designs: for the queen was in such grief, that although urged to give the necessary orders she refused, assuring them that she knew nothing about war. By her command, however, the pagodas that had been found in besieged cities, and in the closets of great generals, were assembled. She ordered them to provide for everything, and then shut herself up in her closet, regarding all the events of life with the utmost indifference.

Magotine's general was the celebrated Punchinello, who knew his business well, and who had a large reserve force, consisting of wasps, cockchafers, and butterflies, who were able to do wonders against a few frogs and light-armed lizards. They had been for a long time in the pay of the pagodas, who were more formidable in name than in valor.

Sometimes Magotine amused herself by watching the fight. Pagodas and pagodinas surpassed themselves, but with a stroke of the wand the fairies destroyed all the superb edifices, and the delightful gardens, woods, meadows, and fountains were buried in the ruins. Queen Laidronette was compelled to become a slave to the most malicious fairy that ever lived. Four or five hundred marionettes brought her to Magotine.

"Madam," said Punchinello, "I venture to present to you the Queen of the Pagodas."

"I have known her for a long while," said Magotine; "she was the cause of an affront I received the day of her birth, and I shall never forget it."

"Alas! madam," said the queen, "I thought you were sufficiently avenged; the gift of ugliness you bestowed on me would have more than satisfied a less vindictive person than yourself."

"How she talks," said the fairy, "just like a newly fledged doctor; your first work shall be to teach my ants philosophy; prepare to give them a lecture every day."

"How am I to manage it, madam?" said the miserable queen; "I do not know philosophy, and if I did, are your ants capable of understanding it?"

"Listen to the logician!" shouted Magotine. "Well, queen, you shall not teach them philosophy, but in spite of yourself, you shall afford the world an example of patience it shall be difficult to imitate."

Then she had iron shoes brought in; they were so tight that Laidronette could not get her feet into them, but she had to put them on all the same ; and the poor queen wept and endured the pain.

"Here," said Magotine, "is a distaff filled with cobweb; in two hours you must spin it as fine as your hair."

"I do not know how to spin," said the queen; "but although it seems impossible, I will endeavour to obey you." She was immediately taken to the depths of a dark grotto, and after leaving her some brown bread and a pitcher of water, the entrance was closed up by a big stone.

When she tried to spin the horrid cobweb, the heavy spindle fell to the ground hundreds and hundreds of times. She had patience enough to pick it up as often, and to begin the task over and over again; but it was always in vain.

"Now," she said, "I perfectly recognise the measure of my misfortune; I am in the power of the implacable Magotine, and she, not satisfied with depriving me of my beauty, wishes to take my life."

She began to weep, going over in her mind the happiness she had enjoyed in the Kingdom of Pagody, and throwing her distaff to the ground: "Let Magotine come when she pleases," she said, "I cannot do what is impossible."

She heard a voice that said: "Ah! queen; your indiscreet curiosity is the cause of all your tears: but I cannot witness the suffering of her I love. I have a friend of whom I have never spoken, the Fairy Protectress; I trust she will be of great use to you."

Three knocks were then heard, and although no one appeared, the cobweb was spun and wound off. At the end of the two hours, Magotine, hoping for a cause of quarrel, ordered the stone to be removed from the entrance, and she went into the grotto, attended by a numerous cortege of marionettes.

"Let us see," said she, "the work of a lazy girl who can neither sew nor spin."

"Madam," said the queen, "I certainly did not know, but I found it necessary to learn."

When Magotine saw the strange circumstance she took the ball of cobweb thread, saying: "You are indeed skilful, and it would be a vast pity not to make use of you. Make nets with this thread, strong enough for catching salmon."

"I beg your pardon," replied she, "but it's scarcely strong enough for flies."

"You are very fond of arguing, my fine friend," said Magotine, "but it is not of the least use." She left the grotto, ordered the big stone to be replaced at the entrance, and assured the queen that if the nets were not finished in two hours she was lost.

"Ah! Fairy Protectress," said the queen, "if it is true that my misfortunes can in any way touch you, do not refuse your aid."

In the same moment the nets were finished. Laidronette was intensely surprised, and thanked in her heart the kind fairy who did so much for her; she thought with pleasure that she doubtless owed such a friend to her husband's love.

"Alas! Green Serpent," she said, "you are very generous to continue loving me after the evil I have done you."

No reply was forthcoming, for Magotine entered, and was greatly astonished to find the nets so industriously wrought, since it was not work for ordinary hands.

"Do you dare to tell me," she said, "that you have woven these nets yourself?"

"I have no friend at your court, madam," said the queen, "and even if I had, I am so closely imprisoned that it would be difficult for any one to speak to me without your permission."

"As you are so clever and skilful, I shall find you very useful in my kingdom."

She at once commanded the fleet to be prepared; all the marionettes were ready to depart. She had the queen fastened in big iron chains, fearing she might through some impulse of despair throw herself into the sea. The unhappy princess was one night deploring her sad fate, when by the light of the moon she perceived Green Serpent quietly approaching the vessel.

"I always fear to alarm you," he said; "although I have no reason to treat you with consideration, you are infinitely dear to me."

"Can you forgive my indiscreet curiosity?" she asked, "and may I tell you without displeasing you?

*"My Serpent! O love! art thou come to me*
*To stay my heart's weary longing for thee?*
*Dear, tender spouse! do I see thee again?*
*Ah! cruel, alas! was solitude's pain!*
*Sorrowful in misery,*
*Weeping I have yearned for thee."*

Serpent replied in these lines:-

*"Hearts apart needs must smart,*
*Weeping duly, loving truly*
*When gods vent their wrath in this world of woe,*
*Wreaking their vengeance with pitiless blow.*
*Torture no worse can they ever devise*
*Than his, who alone in solitude sighs."*

Magotine was not one of those fairies who are sometimes caught napping; the desire of doing evil kept her always wide awake. Thus she did not fail to hear the conversation of King Serpent and his wife. She interposed like a fury.

"Ah, ah!" she said, "you meddle with rhyming and make your laments in the tones of Apollo. Indeed, I am very glad. Proserpina, who is my best friend, has asked me to provide her with some poet on hire. It's not that she lacks them, but she wants more of them. Go then, Green Serpent, finish your penance in her gloomy kingdom, and present my compliments to the charming Proserpina."

The unfortunate serpent immediately departed with long-drawn hisses. He left the queen in the deepest grief; she thought nothing further could possibly happen to her. In her misery she exclaimed:

"By what crime have we displeased you, cruel Magotine? I had scarcely entered the world when your infernal curse deprived me of my beauty and made me hideous. How can you possibly assert that before my reason was developed and I knew myself, I could be guilty of any misdeed? I am sure that the unhappy king you have just sent to Hades is equally innocent; but put an end to it all and let me die now at once; it is the only favor I ask of you."

"If I granted your request you would be too happy," replied Magotine; "you must first fetch water from the inexhaustible spring."

Directly the ships reached the country of the marionettes, cruel Magotine tied a millstone round the queen's neck and ordered her to climb to the top of a mountain far beyond the clouds. Once there she was to gather four-leaved clover, fill her basket with it, and then come down to the depths of the valley and, in a pitcher full of holes, fetch enough of the water of discretion to fill the fairy's big glass.

The queen replied that it was not possible to obey; the millstone was ten times heavier than she was, the broken pitcher could never hold the water, and she could not therefore make up her mind to undertake a thing so impossible.

"If you fail," said Magotine, "be very sure Green Serpent shall suffer."

That threat so greatly alarmed the queen that without considering her complete inability to do what was required of her, she attempted to walk on; but alas! it would have been quite useless had not the Fairy Protectress, whom she summoned, come to her aid.

"This," she said, "is the just reward of your fatal curiosity; you have only yourself to thank for the state into which Magotine has brought you."

But she conveyed Laidronette to the mountain, filled her basket with the four-leaved clover in spite of the dreadful monsters who guarded it and made supernatural efforts to defend it, for by a stroke of the wand the Fairy Protectress made them gentler than lambs.

She did not wait for the thanks of the grateful queen to finish giving her all the aid that lay in her power. She presented her with a little chariot drawn by two white canaries who spoke and sang to perfection. She told her to go down the mountain and to throw her iron shoes at two giants armed with clubs who guarded the spring, and they would fall without offering the least resistance. She was then to give the pitcher to the little canaries who would easily be able to fill it with the water of discretion. Directly they brought it she was to rub her face with it and she would at once become the most beautiful creature in the world.

The fairy advised Laidronette not to remain at the spring, or to climb to the top of the mountain again, but to stop in a pleasant little wood she would find on her road, and stay there for three years. Magotine would think she was all the while engaged in fetching the water in her pitcher, or that one of the numerous dangers of the journey had caused her death.

The queen embraced the Fairy Protectress, and thanked her a hundred times for all her kindness. "But," she added, "neither the happy issue of my journey nor the beauty you promise me can give any joy so long as Green Serpent remains a serpent."

"That will only be until you have lived for three years in the wood," said the fairy, "and have delivered the water and the clover to Magotine."

The queen promised the Fairy Protectress to do everything that she told her. "But, madam," she added, "am I to be three years without hearing anything of Green Serpent?"

"You deserve to be without news of him all your life," said the fairy, "for could there be anything more cruel than to compel him, as you have, to begin his penance all over again?"

The queen replied nothing; her tears and her silence sufficiently testified to her sorrow. She got into the little chariot. The canaries conducted her to the bottom of the valley where the giants guarded the spring of discretion. She promptly took off her iron shoes and threw them at their heads; the giants at once fell lifeless to the ground. The canaries took the pitcher and mended it with such remarkable skill that it did not seem it could ever have been broken. The name of the water made Laidronette desirous of drinking it.

"It will make me," she said, "more prudent and discreet than in the past. Alas! if I had had those qualities, I should be still in the Kingdom of Pagody!"

After she had drunk a long draught, she bathed her face and became so exceedingly beautiful that you would have taken her rather for a goddess than a mortal.

The Fairy Protectress then appeared and said: "You have just done a thing that pleases me vastly; you knew this water had the power of beautifying both your mind and body; I wanted to see which of the two would have the preference. You gave it to your mind and I praise you for it; on account of that action your penance will be shortened by four years."

"Do not lessen my troubles," replied the queen, "I deserve them all; but comfort Green Serpent, who merits none."

"I will do my best," said the fairy, embracing her; "and now since you are so beautiful, I should like you to discontinue the name Laidronette that no longer suits you, and call yourself Queen Discreet."

With these words she disappeared, leaving her a little pair of shoes, so pretty and so beautifully embroidered that she hardly liked to put them on.

When she had re-entered her chariot, holding her pitcher full of water, the canaries took her straight to the wood. There never was a pleasanter place; myrtles and orange trees united their branches to form long sheltered alleys and arbors which the sun could not penetrate. A thousand gently-flowing streams and springs helped to adorn the beauteous spot. But the strangest thing was that all the animals there could speak, and gave the canaries the warmest welcome imaginable.

"We thought," they said, "that you had deserted us."

"The time of our penance is not yet ended," rejoined the canaries, "but the Fairy Protectress bade us bring this queen here; take heed to amuse her as much as possible."

At the same moment she was surrounded by animals of all sorts, who paid her great compliments. "You shall be our queen," they said, "and receive from us every attention and consideration."

"Where am I?" she cried; "by what supernatural power are you able to speak to me?"

One of the canaries, who had remained near her, whispered: "You must know, madam, that certain fairies being on their travels were vexed to see men and women fallen into grievous faults; they thought at first that warning them to change their evil ways would be enough, but that was of no avail, and becoming suddenly very angry indeed, they put them into penance. Those who talked too much they changed into parrots, jays, and hens; lovers and their mistresses into pigeons, canaries, and little dogs; people who were too fond of good eating into pigs; angry persons into lions. In fact, the number of those they put in penance is so great that this wood is populated by them, and you will find here persons of all ranks and dispositions."

"From what you have just told me, my dear little canary," said the queen, "I feel sure I am right in thinking that you are here only for having loved too well."

"Yes, madam," replied the canary, "that is so. I am the son of a Spanish nobleman, and in our country love holds such despotic sway over all hearts that it is not possible to escape it. An ambassador from England arrived at the court; he had a daughter of great beauty, but of an intolerably haughty and cold disposition. Nevertheless, I became attached to her and loved her distractedly; sometimes she seemed sensible of my attentions, while at others she repulsed me so cruelly that I lost patience. One day when she had driven me to despair, a venerable old dame confronted me and blamed me for my weakness; all she could say only served to make me more obstinate, and, perceiving it, she grew angry.

"I condemn you," she said, "to become a canary for three years, and your mistress a wasp." I was at once conscious of the most extraordinary change imaginable; my distress notwithstanding, I could not refrain from flying into the ambassador's garden, to discover the fate of his daughter. But I had scarcely entered it, before I saw a big wasp buzzing four times as loud as any other. I hovered round her with the eagerness of a lover whom nothing could keep away. Several times she tried to sting me. 'If, beautiful wasp,' I said, 'you desire my death, you need not use your sting. Only command me to die, and I will cheerfully obey you.' She vouchsafed no reply, and settled on the flowers, who doubtless suffered for her ill-temper.

"Overwhelmed by her disdain and my own condition, I flew away, following no particular route. I at length reached Paris, one of the most beautiful cities in the world; I was tired, and threw myself on a clump of trees in a walled enclosure, and quite unconscious how it came about, found myself at the door of a cage painted green and ornamented with gold. The furniture and the apartment were of surprising magnificence; a young lady caressed me and spoke to me with a charming gentleness. I did not live long in her room without learning her heart's secret; she was visited by an enraged bully, who, not satisfied with loading her with unjust reproaches, beat her unmercifully, leaving her almost dead in the hands of her attendants. I was in no small degree distressed at witnessing such unworthy treatment, and I was the more displeased to perceive that the more he beat her, the stronger became the charming woman's affection for him.

"I wished night and day that the fairies who turned me into a canary would reduce their ill-assorted love to order. My desire was granted. Just as the lover was beginning his ordinary beating, the fairies suddenly appeared in the room. They loaded him with reproaches, and condemned him to become a wolf; they turned the long-suffering woman into an ewe, and sent them to the wood. As for myself, I easily found means to fly away; I wanted to see the different courts of Europe. I went to Italy, and by chance fell into the hands of a man, who often having business in town, and wishing his wife, of whom he was very jealous, never to see any one, shut her up from morning to night; he, therefore, destined me for the honor of amusing the beautiful captive, but she had other matters to occupy her. A certain neighbor, who had long loved her, was in the habit of coming at evening time down the chimney, sliding from the top to the bottom, and arriving blacker than any demon. The keys, which were in the possession of the jealous husband, only served to make him feel the more secure. I was ever dreading some miserable catastrophe, when the fairies entered by the key-hole, and not a little surprised the loving pair. `Go into penance,' said they, touching their wands; `let the chimney-sweep become a squirrel and the cunning woman a monkey; the husband, who is so careful to keep the keys of his house, shall become a watch-dog for ten years!'

"I should have too many things to relate to you, madam," added the canary, "were I to recount my various adventures. From time to time I was obliged to repair to the wood, and scarcely ever came without finding new animals, for the fairies continued to travel, and people to vex them with their manifold faults, but during the time you dwell here, you can amuse yourself with the adventures of its inhabitants."

Many of them immediately offered to tell her theirs whenever she liked; she thanked them most politely, but desiring rather to reflect than to talk, she sought a solitary spot where she could be alone. As soon as she found one, there arose in it a little palace, and the finest repast imaginable was served her; it was only of fruits, but of very rare fruits, brought by the birds, and as long as she stayed in the wood she wanted for nothing.

Sometimes there were fetes delightful by their oddity: lions danced with lambs, bears told soft tales to doves, and serpents grew gentle for the sake of linnets. A butterfly carried on an intrigue with a panther; in fact, nothing was classified according to its species, and it was not a question of being tiger or sheep, but only of the persons the fairies punished for their faults.

They all loved and adored Queen Discreet; they made her judge in their disputes, and she had absolute power in the little republic. If she had not continually reproached herself for the misfortunes of Green Serpent, she might have endured her own with some sort of patience. But when she thought of his sad condition, she could never forgive herself her indiscreet curiosity. The time for leaving the wood having arrived, she informed her little guides, the faithful canaries, who assured her of a happy return. To avoid farewells and regrets that would have cost her some tears, she slipped away during the night; the affection and respect shown her by these reasoning animals had greatly touched her.

She forgot neither the pitcher full of the water of discretion, nor the basket of clover, nor the iron shoes, and when Magotine believed her dead, she suddenly appeared before her, the millstone round her neck, the iron shoes on her feet, and the pitcher in her hand. The fairy uttered a loud cry, and asked her whence she came.

"Madam," she said, "I spent three years in fetching water in the broken pitcher, and at the end of that time discovered a way to make it stay in."

Magotine burst out laughing, to think of the fatigue the poor queen must have suffered; but looking at her more attentively: "Why, how is this?" she exclaimed;

"Laidronette has become quite charming! How have you come by this beauty?"

The queen told her she had washed in the water of discretion, and so the miracle had come to pass. At this information, Magotine, in despair, threw her pitcher to the ground.

"Oh! power that braves me," she cried, "I can avenge myself. Make ready your iron shoes," she said to the queen, "you must go on my behalf to Proserpina and ask of her the elixir of long life; I always dread falling ill, and even dying. If I had the antidote, I should have no longer cause to fear; take heed therefore not to uncork the bottle or to taste the liquor, for you would thus diminish my share."

This command took the queen completely aback.

"How am I to get to Hades?" she asked; "can those who go there return? Alas! madam, will you never grow tired of persecuting me? Under what star was I born? My sister is far happier than I am; no longer can I believe that the constellations are the same for all."

She began to weep, and Magotine, in triumph to see her shed tears, burst out laughing. "Go, go," she said; "do not delay a moment a journey that is to prove so advantageous to me."

She then put some stale nuts and brown bread into a wallet, and the queen set out, resolved to end her troubles by breaking her head against the first rock she came across.

She walked on some time, unheeding the way she was going, taking first one side and then another, thinking how extraordinary a command it was to send her thus to Hades. When she was tired, she lay down at the foot of a tree and began to dream of poor Green Serpent, thinking no more of her journey. But, suddenly, she saw Fairy Protectress, who said:

"Do you know, beautiful queen, that to rescue your husband from the gloomy abode where, by Magotine's orders, he dwells, you must go to Proserpina?"

"If it was possible I would go even much farther," she replied, "but I do not know how to reach that abode of darkness."

"Here," said the fairy, "is a green branch; strike it on the ground, and speak these verses distinctly."

The queen embraced her generous friend, and then said:

*"Love Love! thine aid I fain would borrow,*
*Who canst the lord of thunder quell,*

*Mitigate my soul's sad sorrow,*
*Ope then for me the path to hell.*
*"You have caused your flame to shine*
*'Neath the world, where dead men dwell.*
*Pluto sighed for Proserpine,*
*Ope then for me the path to hell.*

*"Shall I never see again*
*My faithful loved one by my side?*
*More than mortal is my pain,*
*And death's solace is denied."*

She had hardly finished her prayer, when a young child, beautiful beyond belief, came forth from the depths of a cloud of azure and gold, and sank down at her feet. A crown of flowers encircled his head. By his bow and arrows, the queen recognized that he was Love, and approaching her, he said:

*"No more shall you grieve,*
*For the heavens I leave*
*To wipe the tear-drops away from your eyes.*
*Everything for your sake*
*Will I undertake;*
*Once more shall you see the loved one you prize.*
*Green Serpent again*
*Sweet life shall regain,*
*And with punishment dire his foe we'll chastise."*

The queen, astonished at the brilliance that surrounded Love and enchanted with his promises, cried:

*"To hell will I go, and that hideous place*
*Shall seem to possess a beauteous grace*
*If there once more my love I see,*
*Without whom life hath no charm for me."*

Love, who rarely speaks in prose, after striking the earth three times with his bow, sang these words most beautifully:

*"Earth that knowst Love, grant thou my prayer;*
*Ope wide thy gates, admit us there,*
*Where saddened shores bound darkened lands,*
*And Pluto great the realm commands."*

The earth, obedient, opened wide, and by a dark descent, where there was every need of a guide as brilliant as Love, the queen reached Hades. She dreaded meeting her husband in the form of a serpent; but Love, who sometimes busies himself in doing kindnesses to those who are unfortunate, had foreseen everything, and had already commanded Green Serpent to become what he was before his penance.

However great was Magotine's power, she could do nothing against Love. So the first thing the queen found was her husband, and she had never seen him under so handsome a form; he, likewise had never seen her so beautiful as she had become: however a presentiment and perhaps Love, who was with them, helped them to divine who they were. The queen at once said to him with exquisite tenderness:

*"The cruel Fate that binds thee here*
*Controls me also with her law;*
*My only wish to feel thee near,*
*Thus satisfied for evermore.*

*"Gladly beat our hearts united,*
*Fearlessly in Hades' shades;*
*Joyous love by love requited;*
*For ever vanquished, terror fades."*

The king, transported by the most ardent passion, replied with all that could testify to his enthusiasm and joy; but Love, who likes not to lose time, invited them to approach Proserpina. The queen paid her respects on behalf of the fairy, and begged for the elixir of long life. It was, in fine, the watchword of these good people, and she at once gave her a very badly-corked phial, so that the queen could, if she wished, gratify her curiosity with the greatest ease. Love, who is no novice, set her on her guard against a curiosity that would again prove fatal, and quickly leaving those gloomy regions, the king and queen returned to the light.

Love did not desert them - he conducted them to Magotine, and lest she should see him hid himself in their hearts; his presence, however, inspired the fairy with such kindly feelings that, although she was ignorant of the cause, she received her former victims most cordially, and by a supernatural effort of generosity restored to them the Kingdom of Pagody. There they at once returned and enjoyed in the future as much good fortune as in the past they had suffered disaster and trouble.

*The End.*

*Written by*
*Madame D'Aulnoy (1650-1705)*

*Translated by*
*Miss Lee (1895)*

# III.

# Little Ugly,
# Empress Of The Pagodas

*(Laidronette, impératrice des Pagodes)*

Maurice Ravel

# III.
# Little Ugly, Empress Of The Pagodas

MAURICE RAVEL

Tempo di Marcia ♩ = 116

Picc.
Flt.
Ob.
EH.
2 Cls. in A
2 Bsns.
2 FHs.
Timp. D♯ A♯
Cym.
Tam-tam
Xylo.
Glock (with keyboard)
Cel.
Harp
Vlns. 1 div.
Vlns. 2 div.
Vlas. div.
Ces. div.
Bss. (*)
Piano

1° Mute

C♯ let all the notes ring

Muted

on the fingerboard

pizz.

m.d.

1 2 3 4 5 6 7

(*) four-string bass - tune E-string down ½ step.

1
Solo
Picc.
Flt.
Ob.
EH.
2 Cls.
2 Bsns.
2 FHs.
Cel.
Harp
C♭
1
Muted
pizz.
pp
Vlns. 1
div.
Vlns. 2
div.
Vlas.
div.
Ces.
div.
Bss.
1
pp
Pno.
8
9
10
11
12
13
14

2
Picc.
Flt.
Ob.
EH.
2 Cls.
1°
pp
2 Bsns.
2 FHs.
Cel.
Harp
C♯
2
Vlns. 1 div.
Vlns. 2 div.
Vlas. div.
Ces. div.
Bss.
2
Pno.
mf
15
16
17
18
19
20
21

3
Picc.
Flt.
Ob.
EH.
2 Cls.
2 Bsns.
2 FHs.
Unmuted
a2
Cym.
non troppo
Glock.
Cel.
Harp
Cb
Vlns. 1 div.
Vlns. 2 div.
Vlas. div.
Ces. div.
Bss.
pizz.
arco
remove mutes
Pno.
22
23
24
25
26
27

4
Picc.
Flt.
Ob.
Solo
EH.
2 Cls.
a2
2 Bsns.
2°
2 FHs.
1° +
Cym.
Xylo.
Glock.
Cel.
Harp
Vlns. 1 div.
pizz.
remove mutes
arco
Vlns. 2 div.
Vlas. div.
Ces. div.
Bss.
Pno.
28
29
30
31
32
33
34

5
Picc.
Flt.
Solo
Ob.
EH.
2 Cls.
2 Bsns.
2 FHs.
Muted
Xylo.
Cel.
Harp
Vlns. 1 unis.
pizz.
Vlns. 2 div.
Vlas. unis.
Ces. div.
remove mutes
Bss.
Pno.
35
36
37
38
39
40
41

6
Picc.
Flt.
Ob.
Solo
EH.
p
2 Cls.
p
mf
2 Bsns.
remove mutes
2 FHs.
mf
Cel.
mf
Harp
6
Vlns. 1
p
arco
Vlns. 2
div.
pp
arco
pp
arco
Vlas.
p
pp
arco
Ces.
unis.
pp
pizz.
Bss.
mf
pp
6
Pno.
p
mf
42
43
44
45
46
47
48

Picc.
Flt.
Ob.
EH.
2 Cls.
2 Bsns.
2 FHs.
Cel.
Harp
Vlns. 1
Vlns. 2
Vlas. div.
Ces. div.
Bss.
Pno.
3
p
pp
p
arco
pp
p
gliss.
Ped.
49
50
51
52
53
54
55

7
Picc.
Flt.
Ob.
EH.
2 Cls.
2 Bsns.
2 FHs.
Xylo.
Cel.
Harp
Vlns. 1
div.
Vlns. 2
div.
Vlas.
unis.
Ces.
unis.
Bss.
Pno.
pizz.
pp
p
mp
mf
1°
56
57
58
59
60
61
62

8
Picc.
Flt.
Ob.
EH.
2 Cls.
2 Bsns.
2 FHs.
Xylo.
Cel.
Harp
Vlns. 1
div.
Vlns. 2
div.
Vlas.
div.
Ces.
Bss.
Pno.
pizz.
a2
63
64
65
66
67
68
69

Picc.
Flt.
Ob.
EH.
2 Cls.
2 Bsns.
2 FHs.
T. t.
Cel.
Harp
Vlns. 1
Vlns. 2
Vlas. unis.
Ces.
Bss. div.
Pno.
f
mf
pp
F♯
Muted
arco
70
71
72
73
74
75
76
77
78
79
80
81

9
Flt.
2 Cls.
1° Solo
p
T. t.
Harp
Vlns. 1
Vlns. 2
Vlas.
Ces.
Bss. div.
9
Pno.
espressivo
82
83
84
85
86
87
88
89
90
91

10
2 Cls.
T. t.
Solo
mp
Cel.
p
Harp
Vlns. 1
Vlns. 2
Vlas.
Ces.
Bss. div.
10
ppp
m. d.
m. g.
m. d.
m. g.
Pno.
92
93
94
95
96
97
98
99
100
101

Flt.
2 Cls.
T. t.
Cel.
Harp
Vlns. 1
Vlns. 2
Vlas.
Ces.
Bss. div.
Pno.
11
Solo
pp molto espressivo
Fb
Muted
arco
pp
m. d.
m. g.
102
103
104
105
106
107
108
109
110
111

Flt.
Harp
A♯ G♮
Vlns. 1
Vlns. 2
Vlas.
Ces.
Bss. unis.
Pno.
p
112
113
114
115
116
117
118
119
120
121

12
Flt.
2 Cls.
2 Bsns.
Harp
Vlns. 1
Vlns. 2
Vlas.
Ces.
Bss.
Pno.
p
1°
Gb
pizz.
3
122
123
124
125
126
127
128
129
130
131

13
Flt.
2 Cls.
2 Bsns.
2 FHs.
Timp.
T. t.
Harp
Vlns. 1
Vlns. 2
Vlas.
Ces. div.
Bss. div.
Pno.
pp
a2
pp espressivo
Mute 2°
C♯ F♯ A♭
arco
pizz.
pp prominent and expressive
m. d.
m. g.
132
133
134
135
136
137
138
139
140
141

14
Picc.
Flt.
2 Cls.
2 Bsns.
2 FHs.
Mute
Timp.
T. t.
Xylo.
Cel.
Harp
on the fingerboard
Vlns. 1
div. a 3
Vlns. 2
div. a 3
Vlas.
Ces.
div.
Bss.
div.
Pno.
without accents
142
143
144
145
146
147
148

Picc.
Flt.
Ob.
EH.
2 Cls.
2 Bsns.
2 FHs.
Timp.
T. t.
Xylo.
Cel.
Harp
Vlns. 1
div. a 3
Vlns. 2
div. a 2
Vlas.
div. a 3
Ces.
div.
Bss.
div.
Pno.
pp espressivo
remove mutes
gliss.
normal
div. a 2
on the fingerboard
pizz.
arco
149
150
151
152
153
154
155

15
Picc.
Flt.
Ob.
EH.
2 Cls.
2 Bsns.
2 FHs.
Cym.
non troppo
Glock.
Cel.
Harp
Cb
Vlns. 1 div.
Vlns. 2 div.
Vlas. div.
Ces. div.
Bss. div.
Pno.
pizz.
arco
remove mutes
a2
156
157
158
159
160
161
162

16
Picc.
Flt.
Ob.
Solo
pp
EH.
pp
p
2 Cls.
2°
2 Bsns.
mf
1°
2 FHs.
pp
Xylo.
pp
mf
p
Harp
16
arco
Vlns. 1
div.
remove mutes
arco
pp
Vlns. 2
div.
remove mutes
Vlas.
div.
remove mutes
Ces.
div.
remove mutes
pp
Bss.
unis
16
Pno.
pp
163
164
165
166
167
168
169
170

17
Picc.
Flt.
Solo
Ob.
EH.
Solo
2 Cls.
2 Bsns.
2 FHs.
Muted
Cel.
Harp
17
Vlns. 1
unis.
pizz.
Vlns. 2
div.
pizz.
pizz.
Vlas.
unis.
pizz.
Ces.
unis.
Bss.
arco
17
Pno.
171
172
173
174
175
176
177

18
Picc.
Flt.
Ob.
EH.
2 Cls.
2 Bsns.
2 FHs.
remove mutes
Cel.
Harp
18
Vlns. 1
Vlns. 2
div.
arco
pp
arco
pp
Vlas.
arco
pp
Ces.
arco
pp
pizz.
Bss.
pp
18
Pno.
178
179
180
181
182
183
184

19
Picc.
Flt.
Ob.
EH.
2 Cls.
2 Bsns.
2 FHs.
Xylo.
Cel.
Harp
Fb
arco
pizz.
Vlns. 1 div.
Vlns. 2 div.
Vlas. div.
Ces. div.
Bss.
gliss.
Pno.
185
186
187
188
189
190
191

Picc.
Flt.
Ob.
EH.
2 Cls.
2 Bsns.
2 FHs.
Xylo.
Cel.
Harp
Vlns. 1 div.
Vlns. 2 div.
Vlas. div.
Ces. unis.
Bss.
Pno.
cresc.
mf
mp
ff
1°
pizz.
192
193
194
195
196
197

Picc.
Flt.
Ob.
EH.
2 Cls.
2 Bsns.
2 FHs.
Cym.
1 Cymbal with Bass Drum beater with felt
Xylo.
Glock.
Cel.
Harp
gliss.
Vlns. 1 div.
Vlns. 2 div.
Vlas. div.
Ces. div.
Bss.
Pno.
198
199
200
201
202
203
204

# Practical Analysis

## Little Ugly, Empress Of The Pagodas

Originally titled *Green Serpent*, this is the story of a young king who, through an evil spell, was transformed into a sea-going Green Serpent and a baby princess who was transformed into Little Ugly (Laidronette). The two travel to the land of the Pagodas, the princess by ship and the king under the sea.

Dramatically, this is the "go to" piece for what is generally considered "Chinese" music because of the use of the Pentatonic scale (black keys on the Piano).

One thing that becomes very apparent is that Ravel didn't so much transcribe this movement from the Piano to the Orchestra, as much as he *recomposed* it for orchestra. The Piano is one medium offering X number of choices and opportunities. But when it came to the Orchestra, he had a much greater tonal palette of expression. From my perspective, the Piano part serves more as a sketch score to the larger orchestration.

### Orchestral Setup

Ravel expands his tonal palette by adding to the percussion section: triangle, keyboard glockenspiel, celeste, xylophone, timpani, cymbal, and tam tam. Ravel uses the percussion to help create the oriental sound and feel.

Piccolo
Flute
Oboe
English horn
2 Clarinets in A
2 Bassoons
2 French horns
Timpani
Triangle
Cymbal
Tam Tam
Xylophone
Glockenspiel with keyboard
Celeste
Harp
Violins 1
Violins 2
Violas
Cellos
Basses

## Form

The piece is organized around a series of seven themes. While we have no notes from Ravel, I've named some of them to give a sense of the scene being composed. From the story, it appears to me that this is the presentation of the Pagodas (see pages 63 - 65 in the story), which I've defined as the "What's this?" theme. At bar 69 there's a fanfare, followed by the Green Serpent's theme. Beginning at 109 we have what I've called the Endearment theme.

| | |
|---|---|
| **Bars 1 - 8** | What's this? |
| **Bars 9 - 15** | Entrance of the Pagodas (A) |
| **Bars 16 - 23** | Entrance of the Pagodas ($A^1$) |
| **Bars 24 - 31** | Hail to the Princess (B) |
| **Bars 32 - 37** | Greetings ( C ) |
| **Bars 38 - 55** | Greetings ($C^1$) |
| **Bars 56 - 68** | Ensemble (D) |
| **Bars 69 - 82** | Fanfare (E) |
| **Bars 83 - 108** | Green Serpent Theme (F) |
| **Bars 109 - 122** | Endearment (G) |
| **Bars 123 - 136** | Endearment ($G^1$) |
| **Bars 137 - 156** | Green Serpent Theme (F) |
| **Bars 157 - 164** | Hail to the Princess (B) |
| **Bars 165 - 188** | Pagoda's Theme ($A^1$) |
| **Bars 189 - 201** | Ensemble (D) |
| **Bars 202 - 204** | Finale |

## Melody and the 8 Keys of Professional Orchestration

*Little Ugly* is very much a study of how to break up a melodic line and assign it to different instruments. By looking at the dynamics, you can see that many color combinations work because the instruments are written *p* to *pp*. Where there's *f* and *ff*, you see the most doubling of instruments. Below, the + sign means *unison* while the – sign means *octaves*

| Bar Numbers | Instrument(s) | Which of the 8 Keys | Dynamics |
|---|---|---|---|
| 1 - 8 | Broken melodic line between ½ Cellos, ½ Violas, ½ Violins 2, Bassoon, FH and Flute. Most often ½ Cellos are pizz + Bassoon 1, ½ Violas + Muted FH 1, ½ Violins 2 pizz + Flute. Clusters handled by fingered tremolo reinforced by Harp + Cello. | | *pp, ppp* |
| 9 - 21 | Piccolo | First Key | *pp* |
| 21 - 23 | Flute | First Key | *pp* |
| 24 - 31 | Picc + Flt + Cel; Picc + Flt - Cl 1 + Cl 2 + Glock - Bsn 1 + FH 1 - Bsn 2 + FH 2 | Third Key | *ff to pp, ff to pp* |

| Bar Numbers | Instrument(s) | Which of the 8 Keys | Dynamics |
|---|---|---|---|
| 32 - 37 | Oboe | First Key | *pp* |
| 38 - 41 | Flute | First Key | *p* |
| 42 - 46 | English horn | First Key | *p* |
| 46 - 48 | Flute | First Key | *pp* |
| 48 - 50 | English horn | First Key | *pp* |
| 50 - 52 | Flute | First Key | *pp* |
| 52 - 54 | English horn | First Key | *pp* |
| 54 - 55 | Flute | First Key | *pp* |
| 56 - 60 | Picc - Flt + Cel - Xyl | Third Key | *pp* |
| 60 - 62 | Picc - Flt + Cl 1 + Cel - Xyl | Third Key | *p* |
| 62 - 64 | Picc - Flt + Ob + Cl 1 + Cel - Xyl | Third Key | *mp* |
| 64 - 68 | Picc + Flt + Cel - Ob + Cl + Cel - EH - Xyl | Third Key | *f, ff* |
| 69 | 2 FH + 2 Bsn + 2 Cl + EH + Ob + Flt | Third Key | *ff* |
| 70 - 72 | 2 FH + 2 Bsn + 2 Cl + EH + Ob + Cel + Harp + Harp* | Third Key | *ff* |
| 73 - 76 | 2 FH + 2 Bsn + 2 Cl + Flt + Cel + Harp + Harp + Cellos | Third Key | *ff* |
| 77 - 80 | 2 FH + Flt + Cel + Harp + Harp + Violas | Third Key | *ff* |
| 83 - 92 | Clarinet | First Key | *p* |
| 93 - 108 | Celeste | First Key | *mp* |
| 109 - 137 | Flute | First Key | *pp, p* |
| 137 - 148 | 2 Clarinet | First Key | *pp* |
| 149 - 152 | English horn | First Key | *pp* |
| 153 - 156 | Oboe + Violins 1 | Third Key | *pp* |
| 157 - 164 | Picc + Flt + Cel; Picc + Flt - Cl 1 + Cl 2 + Glock - Bsn 1 + FH 1 - Bsn 2 + FH 2 | Third Key | *ff to pp, ff to pp* |
| 165 - 170 | Oboe | First Key | *pp* |
| 171 - 174 | Flute | First Key | *pp, mf* |
| 175 - 179 | English horn | First Key | *p, mf* |
| 179 - 180 | Flute | First Key | *pp* |

| Bar Numbers | Instrument(s) | Which of the 8 Keys | Dynamics |
|---|---|---|---|
| 181 - 182 | English Horn | First Key | *pp* |
| 183 - 184 | Flute | First Key | *pp* |
| 185 - 186 | English horn | First Key | *pp* |
| 187 - 188 | Flute | First Key | *p* |
| 189 - 192 | Picc - Flt - Xyl | Third Key | *pp* |
| 193 - 195 | Picc - Flt + Cl + Cel - Xyl | Third Key | *p* |
| 195 - 197 | Picc - Flt + Ob + Cl + Cel - Xyl | Third Key | *mp* |
| 198 - 201 | Pic+Flt+Cel - Oboe +Cl + Cel - EH + Xyl | Third Key | *ff* |

## Analysis Comments

In this section, I'm focusing on those aspects of the score that fall into the Fourth Key (Harmonizing Within a Section), and the Sixth Key (Solving Practical Issues). The Fourth and Sixth Keys are most often seen in the background lines and accompaniment. As a result, we'll be looking at broader sections than those shown in the charts above.

## Bars 1 - 8: *What's This?*

To me, knowing the story, this section underscores the sense or feeling of *anticipation*. The strings are divided so as to function like a double string orchestra. Let's look at the scale source and the resultant voicings. It's C#, D#, F#, G#, A#, C#. This is the pentatonic scale, but as you may recognize, it's also the black keys on the Piano. What Ravel does is create closed voicing in clusters that alternate low to high by whole step.

**Voicing 1** = C#, D# - G#, A#
**Voicing 2** = F#, G# - C#, D#

Try playing the Piano part then go back to the orchestral score. The eighth note line in the Piano part is the "cumulative rhythm" which is broken up between the divided strings, Bassoon 1, Flute, and muted French horn.

The clusters are drawn out in the Harp with open strings and muted pitches, and the use of fingered tremolo on the fingerboard (*sur la touche, sul tasto*) with muted strings.

Listen to the optional audio recording and step back. What Ravel has created with the orchestra is a musical effect, or to use a contemporary term from electronica, a kind of ambient background.

What holds it all together through the beginning of bar 24, is the sustained pedal in the muted basses using harmonics. Here, I want to make a comment. I've heard for years among those "in the know" that you don't use mutes on basses. At this writing, most string libraries used in electronic scoring if they have mutes, don't have muted basses because of this oft stated myth. But bar 1 of the *Little Ugly* score says, "Basses, muted." Notice that in the instructions, Ravel's basses were four strings and the instruction is to lower the E string by a half-step. The bass harmonic on C# sounds a C sharp at C#4 (an octave and a half-step above middle C).

## Bars 9 - 23: *Entrance of the Pagodas*

Over this background, the Pagoda's theme enters in the Piccolo moving to the Flute.

## Bars 24 - 31: *Hail to the Princess*

The building blocks for this section are the creative use of the Pentatonic scale and structures using fourths and fifths. In bars 24 and 26, Ravel uses pizzicato in the Violins to accent the off beat. In bars 25 and 26, the clusters are supported with fingered tremolos. The lower strings play the continuing eighth note rhythm.

## Bars 32 - 37: *Greetings*

Look at the background line in the Piano part. This is a standard rhythmic background line not restricted to any one style of music. The melody is performed with this supporting structure. So basically, melody and background. Notice that Ravel moves away from the Pentatonic scale source.

## Bars 38 - 55

From bars 38 - 45 Ravel creates a new 4-part chorale-like structure in contrary motion. From 46 - 55, there's a four-part structure but more a melody over a pad (to use a pop arranging term). In bars 46 - 47 Ravel brings back the chromatic cliché line used in the first movement. Notice the feel created at this march tempo was the tempo of the first movement.

## Bars 56 - 68: *Ensemble*

Back to a Pentatonic scale source. Two-part melody and background line with the background line in a two-feel.

## Bars 69 - 80: *Fanfare*

The dynamic is *f*. In the recording, the fanfare sounds like a standard sized French horn section, but when you look at the score, there are only two French horns.

So how did Ravel create such a strong sound? Through doublings (or what synth programmers call *layering*). Look carefully at what instruments are used to play in unison with the French horns, and in what registers. A unique color is in the Harp (which in the chart I've labeled Harp + Harp*). The left hand plays harmonics (which sound an octave higher) while the right hand plays open pitches. The result is a unison.

## Bars 81 - 108: *Green Serpent Theme*

Sustain in open triad in the strings, background rhythm for motion and melody. The background rhythm is an expansion of bar 32.

## Bars 109 - 136: *Endearment*

The melody in this entire section is performed by the Flute, largely in its high register. In arranging terms, there's melody, sustained background and bass line. At a dynamic of *pp*, the Harp performs the bass line. Even with a sustained background line, the background line follows the melody at bars 113 - 114, 119 - 122.

## Bars 137 - 156: *Green Serpent Theme*

Still melody, sustained background and bass line. But a unique twist: the Timpani catches the bass line. Starting at 142, the Green Serpent theme unites with the Pagoda's theme. An inner rhythmic line of eighth notes in the Harp runs from 142 - 145, but the cumulative rhythm continues in bars 146 - 152. Compare to the sustained harmony and rhythmically, you have 4 against 1 counterpoint. Ravel also brings back the Pentatonic harmony in the Violins and Celeste parts.

## Bars 157 - 164: *Hail to the Princess*

Repeat of the earlier section.

## Bars 165 - 188: *Pagoda's Theme*

Repeat of the earlier section. Some re-orchestration in the strings.

## Bars 189 - 201: *Ensemble*

Repeat of the earlier section. Some re-orchestration, but still melody, sustained background, rhythmic background.

## Bars 202 - 204: *Finale*

Look carefully at how Ravel voices the final chords, especially in the strings with the use of double and triple stops, and the voicing in the woodwinds.

## Electronic Scoring Considerations

This is a very challenging piece to replicate. You need to check:

1. That the full range of the piccolo is available
2. That the muted French horn is available (recorded vs. programmed)
3. How the Harp strings sound in the lower register
4. That the sampled Harp has sampled harmonics
5. For the strings - that on the fingerboard (*sur la touche, sul tasto*) is available
6. Bass harmonics
7. How the Clarinet and Celeste sound in unison in the lower register
8. Xylophone and Glock for range and blending.

Without these devices, the work will suffer in a MIDI mock-up.

# Beauty & The Beast

## A Story by Marie Leprince de Beaumont

### *From "Magasin des Enfans", (1757)*

Once upon a time there lived a merchant who was exceedingly rich. He had six children - three boys and three girls - and being a sensible man he spared no expense upon their education, but engaged tutors of every kind for them. All his daughters were pretty, but the youngest especially was admired by everybody. When she was small she was known simply as "the little beauty," and this name stuck to her, causing a great deal of jealousy on the part of her sisters.

This youngest girl was not only prettier than her sisters, but very much nicer. The two elder girls were very arrogant as a result of their wealth; they pretended to be great ladies, declining to receive the daughters of other merchants, and associating only with people of quality. Every day they went off to balls and theatres, and for walks in the park, with many a gibe at their little sister, who spent much of her time in reading good books.

Now these girls were known to be very rich, and in consequence were sought in marriage by many prominent merchants. The two eldest said they would never marry unless they could find a duke, or at least a count. But Beauty - this, as I have mentioned, was the name by which the youngest was known - very politely thanked all who proposed marriage to her, and said that she was too young at present, and that she wished to keep her father company for several years yet.

Suddenly the merchant lost his fortune, the sole property which remained to him being a small house in the country, a long way from the capital. With tears he broke it to his children that they would have to move to this house, where by working like peasants they might just be able to live.

The two elder girls replied that they did not wish to leave the town, and that they had several admirers who would be only too happy to marry them, notwithstanding their loss of fortune. But the simple maidens were mistaken: their admirers would no longer look at them, now that they were poor. Everybody disliked them on account of their arrogance, and folks declared that they did not deserve pity: in fact, that it was a good thing their pride had had a fall - a turn at minding sheep would teach them how to play the fine lady! "But we are very sorry for Beauty's misfortune," everybody added; "she is such a dear girl, and was always so considerate to poor people: so gentle, and with such charming manners!"

There were even several worthy men who would have married her, despite the fact that she was now penniless; but she told them she could not make up her mind to leave her poor father in his misfortune, and that she intended to go with him to the country, to comfort him and help him to work. Poor Beauty had been very grieved at first over the loss of her fortune, but she said to herself:

"However much I cry, I shall not recover my wealth, so I must try to be happy without it."

When they were established in the country the merchant and his family started working on the land. Beauty used to rise at four o'clock in the morning, and was busy all day looking after the house, and preparing dinner for the family. At first she found it very hard, for she was not accustomed to work like a servant, but at the end of a couple of months she grew stronger, and her health was improved by the work. When she had leisure she read, or played the harpsichord, or sang at her spinning wheel.

Her two sisters, on the other hand, were bored to death; they did not get up till ten o'clock in the morning, and they idled about all day. Their only diversion was to bemoan the beautiful clothes they used to wear and the company they used to keep.

"Look at our little sister," they would say to each other; "her tastes are so low and her mind so stupid that she is quite content with this miserable state of affairs."

The good merchant did not share the opinion of his two daughters, for he knew that Beauty was more fitted to shine in company than her sisters. He was greatly impressed by the girl's good qualities, and especially by her patience - for her sisters, not content with leaving her all the work of the house, never missed an opportunity of insulting her.

They had been living for a year in this seclusion when the merchant received a letter informing him that a ship on which he had some merchandise had just come safely home. The news nearly turned the heads of the two elder girls, for they thought that at last they would be able to quit their dull life in the country. When they saw their father ready to set out they begged him to bring them back dresses, furs, caps, and finery of every kind. Beauty asked for nothing, thinking to herself that all the money which the merchandise might yield would not be enough to satisfy her sisters' demands.

"You have not asked me for anything," said her father.

"As you are so kind as to think of me," she replied, "please bring me a rose, for there are none here."

Beauty had no real craving for a rose, but she was anxious not to seem to disparage the conduct of her sisters. The latter would have declared that she purposely asked for nothing in order to be different from them.

The merchant duly set forth; but when he reached his destination there was a lawsuit over his merchandise, and after much trouble he returned poorer than he had been before. With only thirty miles to go before reaching home, he was already looking forward to the pleasure of seeing his children again, when he found he had to pass through a large wood. Here he lost himself. It was snowing horribly; the wind was so strong that twice he was thrown from his horse, and when night came on he made up his mind he must either die of hunger and cold or be eaten by the wolves that he could hear howling all about him.

Suddenly he saw, at the end of a long avenue of trees, a strong light. It seemed to be some distance away, but he walked towards it, and presently discovered that it came from a large palace, which was all lit up.

The merchant thanked heaven for sending him this help, and hastened to the castle. To his surprise, however, he found no one about in the courtyards. His horse, which had followed him, saw a large stable open and went in; and on finding hay and oats in readiness the poor animal, which was dying of hunger, set to with a will. The merchant tied him up in the stable, and approached the house, where he found not a soul. He entered a large room; here there was a good fire, and a table laden with food, but with a place laid for one only. The rain and snow had soaked him to the skin, so he drew near the fire to dry himself.

"I am sure," he remarked to himself, "that the master of this house or his servants will forgive the liberty I am taking; doubtless they will be here soon."

He waited some considerable time; but eleven o'clock struck and still he had seen nobody. Being no longer able to resist his hunger he took a chicken and devoured it in two mouthfuls, trembling. Then he drank several glasses of wine, and becoming bolder ventured out of the room. He went through several magnificently furnished apartments, and finally found a room with a very good bed. It was now past midnight, and as he was very tired he decided to shut the door and go to bed.

It was ten o'clock the next morning when he rose, and he was greatly astonished to find a new suit in place of his own, which had been spoilt.

"This palace," he said to himself, "must surely belong to some good fairy, who has taken pity on my plight."

He looked out of the window. The snow had vanished, and his eyes rested instead upon arbors of flowers - a charming spectacle. He went back to the room where he had supped the night before, and found there a little table with a cup of chocolate on it.

"I thank you, Madam Fairy," he said aloud, "for being so kind as to think of my breakfast."

Having drunk his chocolate the good man went forth to look for his horse. As he passed under a bower of roses he remembered that Beauty had asked for one, and he plucked a spray from a mass of blooms. The very same moment he heard a terrible noise, and saw a beast coming towards him which was so hideous that he came near to fainting.

"Ungrateful wretch!" said the Beast, in a dreadful voice; "I have saved your life by receiving you into my castle, and in return for my trouble you steal that which I love better than anything in the world - my roses. You shall pay for this with your life! I give you fifteen minutes to make your peace with Heaven."

The merchant threw himself on his knees and wrung his hands. "Pardon, my lord!" he cried; "one of my daughters had asked for a rose, and I did not dream I should be giving offense by picking one."

"I am not called 'my lord,'" answered the monster, "but 'The Beast.' I have no liking for compliments, but prefer people to say what they think. Do not hope therefore to soften me by flattery. You have daughters, you say; well, I am willing to pardon you if one of your daughters will come, of her own choice, to die in your place. Do not argue with me - go! And swear that if your daughters refuse to die in your place you will come back again in three months."

The good man had no intention of sacrificing one of his daughters to this hideous monster, but he thought that at least he might have the pleasure of kissing them once again. He therefore swore to return, and the Beast told him he could go when he wished.

"I do not wish you to go empty-handed," he added; "return to the room where you slept; you will find there a large empty box. Fill it with what you will; I will have it sent home for you."

With these words the Beast withdrew, leaving the merchant to reflect that if he must indeed die, at all events he would have the consolation of providing for his poor children.

He went back to the room where he had slept. He found there a large number of gold pieces, and with these he filled the box the Beast had mentioned. Having closed the latter, he took his horse, which was still in the stable, and set forth from the palace, as melancholy now as he had been joyous when he entered it.

The horse of its own accord took one of the forest roads, and in a few hours the good man reached his own little house. His children crowded round him, but at sight of them, instead of welcoming their caresses, he burst into tears. In his hand was the bunch of roses which he had brought for Beauty, and he gave it to her with these words:

"Take these roses, Beauty; it is dearly that your poor father will have to pay for them."

Thereupon he told his family of the dire adventure which had befallen him. On hearing the tale the two elder girls were in a great commotion, and began to upbraid Beauty for not weeping as they did.

"See to what her smugness has brought this young ingrate," they said; "surely she might strive to find some way out of this trouble, as we do! But oh, dear me, no; her ladyship is so determined to be different that she can speak of her father's death without a tear!"

"It would be quite useless to weep," said Beauty. "Why should I lament my father's death? He is not going to die. Since the monster agrees to accept a daughter instead, I intend to offer myself to appease his fury. It will be a happiness to do so, for in dying I shall have the joy of saving my father, and of proving to him my devotion."

"No, sister," said her three brothers; "you shall not die; we will go in quest of this monster, and will perish under his blows if we cannot kill him."

"Do not entertain any such hopes, my children," said the merchant; "the power of this Beast is so great that I have not the slightest expectation of escaping him. I am touched by the goodness of Beauty's heart, but I will not expose her to death. I am old and have not much longer to live; and I shall merely lose a few years that will be regretted only on account of you, my dear children."

"I can assure you, father," said Beauty, "that you will not go to this palace without me. You cannot prevent me from following you. Although I am young I am not so very deeply in love with life, and I would rather be devoured by this monster than die of the grief which your loss would cause me."

Words were useless. Beauty was quite determined to go to this wonderful palace, and her sisters were not sorry, for they regarded her good qualities with deep jealousy.

The merchant was so taken up with the sorrow of losing his daughter that he forgot all about the box which he had filled with gold. To his astonishment, when he had shut the door of his room and was about to retire for the night, there it was at the side of his bed! He decided not to tell his children that he had become so rich, for his elder daughters would have wanted to go back to town, and he had resolved to die in the country. He did confide his secret to Beauty, however, and the latter told him that during his absence they had entertained some visitors, amongst whom were two admirers of her sisters. She begged her father to let them marry; for she was of such a sweet nature that she loved them, and forgave them with all her heart the evil they had done her.

When Beauty set off with her father the two heartless girls rubbed their eyes with an onion, so as to seem tearful; but her brothers wept in reality, as did also the merchant. Beauty alone did not cry, because she did not want to add to their sorrow.

The horse took the road to the palace, and by evening they espied it, all lit up as before. An empty stable awaited the nag, and when the good merchant and his daughter entered the great hall, they found there a table magnificently laid for two people. The merchant had not the heart to eat, but Beauty, forcing herself to appear calm, sat down and served him. Since the Beast had provided such splendid fare, she thought to herself, he must presumably be anxious to fatten her up before eating her.

When they had finished supper they heard a terrible noise. With tears the merchant bade farewell to his daughter, for he knew it was the Beast. Beauty herself could not help trembling at the awful apparition, but she did her best to compose herself. The Beast asked her if she had come of her own free will, and she timidly answered that such was the case.

"You are indeed kind," said the Beast, "and I am much obliged to you. You, my good man, will depart tomorrow morning, and you must not think of coming back again. Good-bye, Beauty!"

"Good-bye, Beast!" she answered. Thereupon the monster suddenly disappeared.

"Daughter," said the merchant, embracing Beauty, "I am nearly dead with fright. Let me be the one to stay here!"

"No, father," said Beauty, firmly, "you must go tomorrow morning, and leave me to the mercy of Heaven. Perhaps pity will be taken on me."

They retired to rest, thinking they would not sleep at all during the night, but they were hardly in bed before their eyes were closed in sleep. In her dreams there appeared to Beauty a lady, who said to her:

"Your virtuous character pleases me, Beauty. In thus undertaking to give your life to save your father you have performed an act of goodness which shall not go unrewarded."

When she woke up Beauty related this dream to her father. He was somewhat consoled by it, but could not refrain from loudly giving vent to his grief when the time came to tear himself away from his beloved child.

As soon as he had gone Beauty sat down in the great hall and began to cry. But she had plenty of courage, and after imploring divine protection she determined to grieve no more during the short time she had yet to live. She was convinced that the Beast would devour her that night, but made up her mind that in the interval she would walk about and have a look at this beautiful castle, the splendor of which she could not but admire.

Imagine her surprise when she came upon a door on which were the words "Beauty's Room"! She quickly opened this door, and was dazzled by the magnificence of the appointments within.

"They are evidently anxious that I should not be bored," she murmured, as she caught sight of a large bookcase, a harpsichord, and several volumes of music. A moment later another thought crossed her mind. "If I had only a day to spend here," she reflected, "such provision would surely not have been made for me."

This notion gave her fresh courage. She opened the bookcase, and found a book in which was written, in letters of gold:

"Ask for anything you wish: you are mistress of all here."

"Alas!" she said with a sigh, "my only wish is to see my poor father, and to know what he is doing."

As she said this to herself she glanced at a large mirror. Imagine her astonishment when she perceived her home reflected in it, and saw her father just approaching. Sorrow was written on his face; but when her sisters came to meet him it was impossible not to detect, despite the grimaces with which they tried to simulate grief, the satisfaction they felt at the loss of their sister. In a moment the vision faded away, yet Beauty could not but think that the Beast was very kind, and that she had nothing much to fear from him.

At midday she found the table laid, and during her meal she enjoyed an excellent concert, though the performers were invisible. But in the evening, as she was about to sit down at the table, she heard the noise made by the Beast, and quaked in spite of herself.

"Beauty," said the monster to her, "may I watch you have your supper?"

"You are master here," said the trembling Beauty.

"Not so," replied the Beast; "it is you who are mistress; you have only to tell me to go, if my presence annoys you, and I will go immediately. Tell me, now, do you not consider me very ugly?"

"I do," said Beauty, "since I must speak the truth; but I think you are also very kind."

"It is as you say," said the monster; "and in addition to being ugly, I lack intelligence. As I am well aware, I am a mere beast."

"It is not the way with stupid people," answered Beauty, "to admit a lack of intelligence. Fools never realize it."

"Sup well, Beauty," said the monster, "and try to banish dullness from your home, for all about you is yours, and I should be sorry to think you were not happy."

"You are indeed kind," said Beauty. "With one thing, I must own, I am well pleased, and that is your kind heart. When I think of that you no longer seem to be ugly."

"Oh yes," answered the Beast, "I have a good heart, right enough, but I am a monster."

"There are many men," said Beauty, "who make worse monsters than you, and I prefer you, notwithstanding your looks, to those who under the semblance of men hide false, corrupt, and ungrateful hearts."

The Beast replied that if only he had a grain of wit he would compliment her in the grand style by way of thanks; but that being so stupid he could only say he was much obliged.

Beauty ate with a good appetite, for she now had scarcely any fear of the Beast. But she nearly died of fright when he put this question to her:

"Beauty, will you be my wife?"

For some time she did not answer, fearing lest she might anger the monster by her refusal. She summoned up courage at last to say, rather fearfully, "No, Beast!"

The poor monster gave forth so terrible a sigh that the noise of it went whistling through the whole palace. But to Beauty's speedy relief the Beast sadly took his leave and left the room, turning several times as he did so to look once more at her. Left alone, Beauty was moved by great compassion for this poor Beast. "What a pity he is so ugly," she said, "for he is so good."

Beauty passed three months in the palace quietly enough. Every evening the Beast paid her a visit, and entertained her at supper by a display of much good sense, if not with what the world calls wit. And every day Beauty was made aware of fresh kindnesses on the part of the monster. Through seeing him often she had become accustomed to his ugliness, and far from dreading the moment of his visit, she frequently looked at her watch to see if it was nine o'clock, the hour when the Beast always appeared.

One thing alone troubled Beauty; every evening, before retiring to bed, the monster asked her if she would be his wife, and seemed overwhelmed with grief when she refused. One day she said to him:

"You distress me, Beast. I wish I could marry you, but I cannot deceive you by allowing you to believe that that can ever be. I will always be your friend - be content with that."

"Needs must," said the Beast. "But let me make the position plain. I know I am very terrible, but I love you very much, and I shall be very happy if you will only remain here. Promise that you will never leave me."

Beauty blushed at these words. She had seen in her mirror that her father was stricken down by the sorrow of having lost her, and she wished very much to see him again.

"I would willingly promise to remain with you always," she said to the Beast, "but I have so great a desire to see my father again that I shall die of grief if you refuse me this boon."

"I would rather die myself than cause you grief," said the monster. "I will send you back to your father. You shall stay with him, and your Beast shall die of sorrow at your departure."

"No, no," said Beauty, crying; "I like you too much to wish to cause your death. I promise you I will return in eight days. You have shown me that my sisters are married, and that my brothers have joined the army. My father is all alone; let me stay with him one week."

"You shall be with him tomorrow morning," said the Beast. "But remember your promise. All you have to do when you want to return is to put your ring on a table when you are going to bed. Good-bye, Beauty!" As usual, the Beast sighed when he said these last words, and Beauty went to bed quite downhearted at having grieved him.

When she woke the next morning she found she was in her father's house. She rang a little bell which stood by the side of her bed, and it was answered by their servant, who gave a great cry at sight of her. The good man came running at the noise, and was overwhelmed with joy at the sight of his dear daughter. Their embraces lasted for more than a quarter of an hour. When their transports had subsided, it occurred to Beauty that she had no clothes to put on; but the servant told her that she had just discovered in the next room a chest full of dresses trimmed with gold and studded with diamonds. Beauty felt grateful to the Beast for this attention, and having selected the simplest of the gowns she bade the servant pack up the others, as she wished to send them as presents to her sisters. The words were hardly out of her mouth when the chest disappeared. Her father expressed the opinion that the Beast wished her to keep them all for herself, and in a trice dresses and chest were back again where they were before.

When Beauty had dressed she learned that her sisters, with their husbands, had arrived. Both were very unhappy. The eldest had wedded an exceedingly handsome man, but the latter was so taken up with his own looks that he studied them from morning to night, and despised his wife's beauty. The second had married a man with plenty of brains, but he only used them to pay insults to everybody - his wife first and foremost.

The sisters were greatly mortified when they saw Beauty dressed like a princess, and more beautiful than the dawn. Her caresses were ignored, and the jealousy which they could not stifle only grew worse when she told them how happy she was. Out into the garden went the envious pair, there to vent their spleen to the full.

"Why should this brat be happier than we are?" each demanded of the other; "are we not much nicer than she is?"

"Sister," said the elder, "I have an idea. Let us try to persuade her to stay here longer than the eight days. Her stupid Beast will fly into a rage when he finds she has broken her word, and will very likely devour her."

"You are right, sister," said the other; "but we must make a great fuss over her if we are to make the plan successful."

With this plot decided upon they went upstairs again, and paid such attention to their little sister that Beauty wept for joy. When the eight days had passed the two sisters tore their hair, and showed such grief over her departure that she promised to remain another eight days.

Beauty reproached herself, nevertheless, with the grief she was causing to the poor Beast; moreover, she greatly missed not seeing him. On the tenth night of her stay in her father's house she dreamed that she was in the palace garden, where she saw the Beast lying on the grass nearly dead, and that he upbraided her for her ingratitude. Beauty woke up with a start, and burst into tears.

"I am indeed very wicked," she said, "to cause so much grief to a Beast who has shown me nothing but kindness. Is it his fault that he is so ugly, and has so few wits? He is good, and that makes up for all the rest. Why did I not wish to marry him? I should have been a good deal happier with him than my sisters are with their husbands. It is neither good looks nor brains in a husband that make a woman happy; it is beauty of character, virtue, kindness. All these qualities the Beast has. I admit I have no love for him, but he has my esteem, friendship, and gratitude. At all events I must not make him miserable, or I shall reproach myself all my life." With these words Beauty rose and placed her ring on the table.

Hardly had she returned to her bed than she was asleep, and when she woke the next morning she saw with joy that she was in the Beast's palace. She dressed in her very best on purpose to please him, and nearly died of impatience all day, waiting for nine o'clock in the evening. But the clock struck in vain: no Beast appeared. Beauty now thought she must have caused his death, and rushed about the palace with loud despairing cries. She looked everywhere, and at last, recalling her dream, dashed into the garden by the canal, where she had seen him in her sleep. There she found the poor Beast lying unconscious, and thought he must be dead. She threw herself on his body, all her horror of his looks forgotten, and, feeling his heart still beat, fetched water from the canal and threw it on his face.

The Beast opened his eyes and said to Beauty: "You forgot your promise. The grief I felt at having lost you made me resolve to die of hunger; but I die content since I have the pleasure of seeing you once more."

"Dear Beast, you shall not die," said Beauty; "you shall live and become my husband. Here and now I offer you my hand, and swear that I will marry none but you. Alas, I fancied I felt only friendship for you, but the sorrow I have experienced clearly proves to me that I cannot live without you."

Beauty had scarce uttered these words when the castle became ablaze with lights before her eyes: fireworks, music - all proclaimed a feast. But these splendors were lost on her: she turned to her dear Beast, still trembling for his danger.

Judge of her surprise now! At her feet she saw no longer the Beast, who had disappeared, but a prince, more beautiful than Love himself, who thanked her for having put an end to his enchantment. With good reason were her eyes riveted upon the prince, but she asked him nevertheless where the Beast had gone.

"You see him at your feet," answered the prince. "A wicked fairy condemned me to retain that form until some beautiful girl should consent to marry me, and she forbade me to betray any sign of intelligence. You alone in all the world could show yourself susceptible to the kindness of my character, and in offering you my crown I do but discharge the obligation that I owe you."

In agreeable surprise Beauty offered her hand to the handsome prince, and assisted him to rise. Together they repaired to the castle, and Beauty was overcome with joy to find, assembled in the hall, her father and her entire family. The lady who had appeared to her in her dream had had them transported to the castle.

"Beauty," said this lady (who was a celebrated fairy), "come and receive the reward of your noble choice. You preferred merit to either beauty or wit, and you certainly deserve to find these qualities combined in one person. It is your destiny to become a great queen, but I hope that the pomp of royalty will not destroy your virtues. As for you, ladies," she continued, turning to Beauty's two sisters, "I know your hearts and the malice they harbor. Your doom is to become statues, and under the stone that wraps you round to retain all your feelings. You will stand at the door of your sister's palace, and I can visit no greater punishment upon you than that you shall be witnesses of her happiness. Only when you recognize your faults can you return to your present shape, and I am very much afraid that you will be statues for ever. Pride, ill-temper, greed, and laziness can all be corrected, but nothing short of a miracle will turn a wicked and envious heart."

In a trice, with a tap of her hand, the fairy transported them all to the prince's realm, where his subjects were delighted to see him again. He married Beauty, and they lived together for a long time in happiness the more perfect because it was founded on virtue.

*The End.*

*Written by*
*Marie Leprince de Beaumont (1711-1780)*

*Translated by*
*A. E. Johnson (1921)*

# IV.

# Dialogue Between Beauty & The Beast

*(La Belle et la Bête)*

Maurice Ravel

# IV.
# Dialogue Between Beauty & The Beast

2 Flts.
2 Obs.
2 Cls.
Bsn.
2 FHs.
Harp
Vlns. 1
Vlns. 2
Vlas.
Ces.
Bss.
Pno.
1
1°
pp
arco
m.g.
9
10
11
12
13
14
15
16
17
18

2 Flts.
2 Cls.
Harp
Vlns. 1
Vlns. 2
Vlas.
Ces.
Bss.
Pno.
pp
pizz.
p
arco
C.B. a 5 strings
m.d.
19
20
21
22
23
24
25
26
27
28

2 Flts.
2 Obs.
2 Cls.
Bsn.
2 FHs.
Harp
Vlns. 1
Vlns. 2
Vlas.
Ces.
Bss.
Pno.
a2
mf
1°
pp
p
pizz.
arco
m.g.
29
30
31
32
33
34
35
36
37
38

2 Flts.
2 Cls.
Bsn.
2 FHs.
Harp
Vlns. 1
Vlns. 2
Vlas.
Ces. div.
Bss.
Pno.
pp
p
1°
Mute
pizz.
very short
ppp
39
40
41
42
43
44
45
46
47
48

2
2 Flts.
2 Obs.
2 Cls.
Bsn.
CBsn.
Solo
2 FHs.
2nd remove mute
1° +
Bass Drum beater with felt
let ring
Cym.
B.D.
Harp
(F♭ G♭ A♭ B♭)
Vlns. 1
remove mute
Vlns. 2
remove mute
Vlas.
pizz.
arco on the fingerboard
Ces. div.
Bss. div.
Pno.
Muted
a little prominent
49
50
51
52
53
54
55
56
57
58
59

2 Flts.
2 Obs.
2 Cls.
Bsn.
CBsn.
2 FHs.
Cym.
B.D.
Harp
Vlns. 1
Vlns. 2
Vlas. div.
Ces. div.
Bss. div.
Pno.
pizz.
arco on the fingerboard
mf
p
pp
1°
60
61
62
63
64
65
66
67
68
69

3
1° Solo
2 Flts.
p molto espressivo
2 Obs.
1° Solo
pp
molto espressivo
CBsn.
p
Vlns. 1
arco
pp
Vlns. 2
arco
pp
Vlas.
unis. remove mutes
pp normal
Ces.
unis. normal
pp
p
remove mutes
Bss.
unis.arco
pp
p
remove mutes
pp
molto espressivo
Pno.
p
pp
70
71
72
73
74
75
76
77
78

Animato
poco
2 Flts.
2 Obs.
1° Solo
2 Cls.
Bsn.
CBsn.
Harp
(FA♭)
(C♭ D♭)
Vlns. 1
Vlns. 2
Vlas.
Ces.
Bss.
Pno.
m.g.
79
80
81
82
83
84
85
86
87

a
poco
2 Flts.
2 Obs.
2 Cls.
a2
Bsn.
CBsn.
2 FHs.
1°
Harp
E♭ G♮ A♮
C♮ G♭ A♭
Vlns. 1
Vlns. 2
div.
Vlas.
Ces.
Bss.
Pno.
m.d.
m.g.
88
89
90
91
92
93
94
95
96

Vivace assai
Rall.
2 Flts.
a2
f
ff
2 Obs.
2 Cls.
Bsn.
CBsn.
2 FHs.
Harp
C♭ F♯ G♮
C♮ D♮
Vlns. 1
Vlns. 2
unis.
Vlas.
p
Ces.
Bss.
Pno.
m.d
m.g.
97
98
99
100
101
102
103
104
105

4 Primo Tempo
2 Flts.
2 Obs.
2 Cls.
Bsn.
CBsn.
2 FHs.
Harp
Vlns. 1
Vlns. 2
Vlas.
Ces.
Bss.
Pno.
pp espressivo
Solo
1° Mute
F♮ A♮
Primo Tempo
Muted
pizz.
arco
a little prominent
106
107
108
109
110
111
112
113
114
115

2 Flts.
2 Obs.
1°
2 Cls.
1°
pp
Bsn.
CBsn.
pp
pp
2 FHs.
Harp
Vlns. 1
remove mutes
Vlns. 2
remove mutes
Vlas.
Ces.
pizz.
p
arco
Bss.
Muted pizz.
pp
arco
mp
sul D
p
p
Pno.
m.g.
m.d.
pp
116
117
118
119
120
121
122
123
124
125

5
2 Flts.
1°
pp
p espressivo
2 Obs.
pp espressivo
2 Cls.
Bsn.
p
CBsn.
pp
p
mf
2 FHs.
Harp
D♮ E♭ F♮ A♮ B♭
Vlns. 1
pizz.
Vlns. 2
remove mutes
Vlas.
arco
Ces.
Bss.
C.B. a 5 strings
Pno.
m.d.
m.g.
f
126
127
128
129
130
131
132
133
134
135
136

2 Flts.
2 Obs.
2 Cls.
Bsn.
CBsn.
2 FHs.
Cym.
Harp
Vlns. 1
Vlns. 2
Vlas.
Ces.
Bss.
Pno.
a2
1°
arco
div.
remove mutes
Animato poco a poco
Vivo
E♮
A♭
B♮
137
138
139
140
141
142
143
144
145

6
Primo Tempo(Poco piú lento)
2º change to Piccolo
2 Flts.
Trg.
Harp
C♮ A♮
gliss.
Vln. Solo
Unmuted
pp molto espressivo
Vlns. 1
Vlns. 2
Muted
Vlas.
Muted
Ces.
Muted
Bss.
Pno.
glissando
pp molto espressivo
146
147
148
149
150
151
152
153
154

Rall.
Piú lento
Picc.
2 Cls.
Bsn.
CBsn.
2 FHs.
Harp
Vln. Solo
Vlns. 1
Vlns. 2
Vlas.
Cello Solo
Ces.
Bss.
Pno.
pp
1°
Mute
sul A
sul G
pizz.
Unmuted
p molto espressivo
Quasi lento
p expressive and prominent
155
156
157
158
159
160
161
162
163

Rall.
Picc.
Flt.
pp
2 Cls.
Bsn.
Cbsn.
2 FHs.
pp
Harp
pp
ppp
Mutes
div. a 4
div. a 2
Vlns. 1
pp
pp die to nothing
pizz.
div. a 4
arco
Vlns. 2
div. a 4
arco
Vlas.
Cello Solo
Mute
div. a 3
unis.
Ces.
die to nothing
arco
Bss.
Pno.
ppp
164
165
166
167
168
169
170
171
172

# Practical Analysis

## Dialogue Between Beauty & The Beast

After many listens, you get the sense that this could have been a scene from an old MGM musical. The coloration is very subtle (something you only pick up when hearing it performed live), as some of that subtlety is lost when listening on CD or MP3.

What comes across is that this is an amazing danceable piece, and you can see why it was later expanded to become a complete ballet.

The scene starts at the second time in which Beast asks Beauty to marry him. Her answer is no, that the best they can ever be is friends. Since we have no notes from Ravel on this, I've labeled bar 86 the start of the C section, which I've labeled *Anguish* as the waltz pattern and the melody are darkened harmonically. However, there is general agreement that at bar 148, Beauty accepts Beast's marriage proposal, and there we hear his transformation into a prince who is as handsome on the outside as he is on the inside.

### Orchestral Setup

2 Flutes
2 Oboes
2 Clarinets in Bb
Bsn
CBsn
2 French Horns
Trg
Cymbal
Bass Drum
Harp
Violins 1
Violins 2
Violas
Cellos
Basses

### Overall Form

I'm defining the form as A B $A^1$ C A C B.

**A** is *Beauty's Theme* - a 2-part melody with development, no bridge.

**B** is *Beast's Theme* - which is basically a motive repeated at various intervals. It functions more as a counterline than an actual second theme.

**Bars 1 - 48** Beauty's Theme (A)
**Bars 49 - 69** Beast's Theme (B)
**Bars 70 - 85** Beauty's Theme (A[1])
**Bars 86 - 101** Anguish - development of Beauty's theme (C)
**Bars 107 - 128** Beauty's Theme restated (A)
**Bars 129 - 146** Anguish restated (C)
**Bars 147 - 172** Beast's Theme - acceptance of marriage proposal, Beast turns into handsome Prince (B)

## Melody and the 8 Keys of Professional Orchestration

There are two themes, one for Beauty (the main theme) and a second theme for Beast. Compositionally, Ravel states each theme independently. Then, the themes are combined together. First, at a distance of two bars, then one bar, then concurrently.

### *Beauty*

Below, the + sign means *unison* while the – sign means *octaves*

| Bar Numbers | Instrument(s) | Which of the 8 Keys | Dynamics |
|---|---|---|---|
| 1 - 48 | Clarinet | First Key | *pp* |
| 70 - 77 | Flute | First Key | *p* |
| 78 - 85 | Oboe | First Key | *pp* |
| 86 - 89 | Clarinet | First Key | *p* |
| 90 - 93 | Violins 1 | First Key | *p* |
| 94 - 95 | Flt + Oboe – Flt + Oboe | Third Key | *mf* |
| 96 - 97 | Vlns 1 + Flt 1 – Vlas + Flt 2 | Third Key | *mf* |
| 98 - 101 | Vlns 1 + 2 Flts – Vlas + 2 Cls | Third Key | *f* |
| 102 - 106 | Vlns 1 + 2 Flts + 2 Cls | Third Key | *ff to p* |
| 107 - 128 | Clarinet | First Key | *pp* |
| 129 - 132 | Oboe | First Key | *pp* |
| 133 - 136 | 1 Flt + 1 Cl | Second Key | *p* |
| 137 - 138 | 1 Flt + 1 Oboe | Second Key | *p* |
| 139 - 145 | Vlns 1 + 2 Flts – Vlas + 2 Cls | Third Key | *mf to ff* |
| 148 - 159 | Solo Violin | First Key | *pp* |
| 160 - 171 | Piccolo + Harp | Third Key | *p to pp* |

## *Beast*

When we get to the Beast theme, we have a study of the Contrabassoon, Basses and Cellos. For blending with the Contrabassoon, the Basses are in the very high register. Remember, the + sign means *unison* while the – sign means *octaves*.

| Bar Numbers | Instrument(s) | Which of the 8 Keys | Dynamics |
|---|---|---|---|
| 1 - 48 | None | | |
| 49 - 93 | Contrabassoon | First Key | *p, mf* |
| 94 | CBsn + Basses | Second Key | *mp* |
| 95 | Bsn + Bass | First Key | *f* |
| 96 - 103 | Bsn + Cellos | First Key | *f to ff* |
| 107 - 131 | Contrabassoon | First Key | *pp* |
| 132 - 136 | CBsn + Basses (sustain) | First Key | *p, mf* |
| 137 - 138 | Bsn + Basses | First Key | *p* |
| 139 - 145 | Bsn + Cellos | First Key | *p to ff* |
| 146 - 172 | None | | |

## Chart of String Devices

Before getting into more detail, I created this chart showing the string devices used in this movement. In looking at Ravel's style, we want to discover where the strings were open and where were they muted and what dramatic impact that has. Then, when Ravel divides the strings, what other instruments, if any, are doubled with them? What devices are used when the strings are open vs muted? Then look at the basses under Muted. The general consensus is that basses aren't muted in the orchestra, as a result, you don't find any sample libraries with muted basses. However, looking at the chart below, Ravel very clearly uses muted basses! And you'll see quite a few techniques used by Ravel with the muted basses to create very interesting colors and combinations.

| | Open | Muted | Divisi | Pizz | Harmonics | On the Fingerboard | Fingered Tremolo |
|---|---|---|---|---|---|---|---|
| **Vlns 1** | 70 - 108, 129 - 145 | 1 - 69, 108 - 121 | 167 - 172 | 31 - 34, 43 - 48, 129 - 136 | Solo, open, 148 - 159 | | |
| **Vlns 2** | 70 - 108, 129 - 145 | 1 - 69, 108 - 121 | 96 - 101, 139 - 144 167 - 172 | 31 - 34, 43 - 48, 129 - 136 | | | |
| **Violas** | 78 - 109, 129 - 145 | 1 - 69, 110 - 128, 148 - 172 | 167 - 172 | 32 - 34, 60 - 63, 129 - 132, 163 - 166 | | 64 - 69 | 64 - 69 |
| **Cellos** | 86 - 109, 139 - 145 | 1 - 85, 110 - 136, 148 - 172 | 53 - 58, 167 - 172 | 23, 49 - 52, 60 - 63, 110 - 113 | 47 - 48, 114 - 118, | 53 - 58, 64 - 69 | 53 - 58, 64 - 69 |
| **Basses** | 78 - 117, 128 - 172 | 1 - 77, 117 - 126 | 53 - 58 | 5 - 16, 27 - 53, 60 - 64, 110 - 119, 163 - 165 | 102 - 104, 128 - 132 | 53 - 58 | 53 - 58 |

## Orchestrating a Waltz

Amidst this look at devices and combinations, we must be mindful that Ravel is orchestrating a waltz. So we have theme and counter theme over a waltz background. Through the charts, we've notated how Ravel orchestrated the two main themes. Now we need to see how Ravel orchestrated the waltz accompaniment.

## Bars 1 - 48: *Beauty's Theme*

What makes these 48 bars so spectacular is the amount of thinking that Ravel put into creating the very subtle combinations in this section using Keys 3 (combining instruments from other orchestral sections) and 5 (combining instruments from other orchestral sections in 3-part harmony or more). For the melody, we have the purity of the solo instrument. For the accompaniment, we have subtle color combinations. For those working with hardware or software synthesizers, the Third Key is the equal to "layering" two sounds together to create a new one. Starting in the first movement, we saw the sonic care Ravel took in blending the pizzicato violas with the muted French horn and the color that was achieved by combining them in that specific range.

Such "layering" comes from listening to the extreme and the astonishing mental practice of imagining those colors in combination. What we composers should draw from this is that rather than just dashing off the score, Ravel gave himself the gift of time to think through and conceptualize each color.

### Role of The Harp

The Harp is the core of these first 48 bars. If we were to think of this waltz rhythm as *oom-pahhh, oom-pahh*, then the left hand is playing the *oom* (the bass line), while the right hand, playing mostly thirds, is playing the *pahh*. Let's see how Ravel handles the doublings for the accompaniment.

**Bars 1 - 4.** From bars 1 - 4, rather than play the bass line open, it's played with harmonics (sounding an octave higher). Look at the muted Violas. They play the sustained bass line under two bars so when the bow touches the string, there's barely a trace of the accent to signal the accented one (*oom*). How does Ravel setup the accent? With the plucked bass in the left hand of the Harp. So Ravel doubles muted Violas and the Harp playing harmonics at a dynamic of *pp*.

The *pahh* is the doubling of the two Flutes with the Harp at a dynamic of *pp*.

**Bars 5 - 8.** The *oom* changes orchestration. Instead of the Harp with harmonics, Ravel uses a sustained muted Cello, with pluck handled by the muted Basses in their very high register. For the *pahh*, the Harp is doubled by the muted Violins 1 and 2 playing at a dynamic of *pp*.

Let's sit back and think for a moment. In bars 1 - 4, 10 muted Violas doubled the Harp playing harmonics. In bars 5 - 8, roughly 24 Violins are doubling the Harp at a dynamic of *pp*. This tells you the delicacy by which the strings are playing so that they're blending rather than overpowering.

**Bars 9 - 12.** The *oom* is with the open Harp doubled by the muted Violas. The *pahh* is the Harp doubled by Clarinet 2 and Bassoon 1.

**Bars 13 - 16.** This is a little trickier. We'll do the *oom-pahh* first. The *oom* is handled by the Harp, sustained Cellos, and the pizzicato Bass (for the accented one). The *pahh* is now three-part harmony. The Harp is doubled by the Oboe, Bassoon and solo French horn. Very subtle. The three-part harmony is created from the two-voice part in the Piano part plus an added harmony part created from the melody.

Now look at the strings as a section. Violins and Violas double the right hand Harp part, with this exception. They play on the *oom* (beat one). So as this harmony repeats on the *pahh* with the mini-woodwind ensemble, it's a subtle echo effect. In synth language, the strings here are playing a *pad*.

These colors are possible because the dynamic is *pp*.

**Bars 17 - 23.** Basses and the Harp perform the sustained bass line (*oom*). The Basses sustain while the Harp supplies the accent on beat one. The inner line (*pahh*) with a filler harmony part is handled with Flute 1 being doubled by the muted Violas. Violins 1 and 2 catch the inner harmony line and filler.

**Bars 24 - 26.** This section is a repeat but with subtle changes. The *oom* is once again handled by the Harp with harmonics doubled by the Violas. That's 24 - 26. The *pah* is assigned to the Harp doubled by the Flutes. Dynamic continues at *pp*.

**Bars 27 - 30.** At 27, the *oom* moves to the Cellos doubled by the pizzicato Basses. The *pah* is the Harp doubled by Violins 1 and 2.

**Bars 31 - 34.** The *oom* is assigned to the sustained Bassoon doubled by the pizzicato Bass. For the first time, the Harp drops out handling the *pahh*. Ravel assigns it to Bassoon 1 and the two French horns. For an added "lilt" on beat 2, Violin 1 plays the top line of the chord (see the Piano part) as pizzicato. While Violin 1 plays, the lower harmony parts are played with Violins 2 alternating with the Violas playing close position triple stops.

**Bars 35 - 48.** We're now into the final phrase of Beauty's theme. For the *oom*, at 35, the left hand of the Harp is doubled by the muted Cellos. For the *pah*, the triad in the right hand of the Harp is doubled by Flute lead over the two French horns. Also at 35, Violins 1 and 2, plus Violas double the right hand Harp part (but on the beat creating the echo effect I pointed out earlier) along with the Cellos on the bass line. Look carefully at Violins 1, Violins 2 and Violas, to see how Ravel at one point outlines the melody then, as in *Little Tom Thumb*, has the woodwind lead over the string ensemble. The waltz feel continues between the Harp plus Oboe and French horns in bars 35 - 36. At bar 40 - 48, notice how the waltz feel has been moved largely to the full string ensemble.

## Bars 49 - 69: *Beast's Theme*

**Bars 49 - 52.** Cellos and Basses are divided but also in unison (2nd Key). Looking at this from a jazz perspective, I see the chord for 49 - 50 being Eb7#11, G2/B at 51, back to Eb7#11 at 52.

**Bars 53 - 69.** Looking at the Piano part, bars 53 and following could be analyzed as E713 omit 5/E on beat 2 and Bb$^{ADD9}$/E on beat 3. This illustrates Ravel's use of chord progression by tritone. However, in the orchestration, we see a much different story. When everything is transposed back to concert pitch, we see a harmony that some might look at as polytonal, but what I see as an altered Mixolydian E scale. As I read it, this is an E7b9#11$^{ADD13}$ with the scale source spelled as E F G# A# B C# D E.

Look carefully at the lower strings. The Basses and Harp pluck the bottom E which is doubled by the sustained Contrabassoon.

On beat 2, the divided Basses play G# and A# as a fingered tremolo while the divided Cellos play the D and E as a fingered tremolo. In jazz theory, the 3rd and 7th define the chord. So we have E, G#, D (E7), plus the A# (#11) and E. Looking carefully at the structure, the chord is voiced so that in the Basses and Cellos, the tritone is sounded delicately.

**From 60 - 69,** the pattern is repeated but up a whole step.

## Electronic Scoring Considerations

I have two considerations here. First, is that the Contrabassoon sound full, especially in the lower register.

Second, the strings are pretty much divisi throughout the piece, so great care must be taken for balancing and matching timbres. See page 149 for a list of the string techniques used. At this writing, no single library has all of these articulations. So you must mix and match.

As mentioned previously, if a library says it has muted strings, you need to find out if the strings were *recorded* muted, or were recorded open and *programmed* to sound muted.

# The Fairy Garden

*FROM*

## *"The Sleeping Beauty In The Woods"*

## A Story by Charles Perrault

### *From "Contes du temps passé", (1697)*

At the end of a hundred years the throne had passed to another family from that of the sleeping princess. One day the king's son chanced to go a-hunting that way, and seeing in the distance some towers in the midst of a large and dense forest, he asked what they were. His attendants told him in reply the various stories which they had heard. Some said there was an old castle haunted by ghosts, others that all the witches of the neighborhood held their revels there. The favorite tale was that in the castle lived an ogre, who carried thither all the children whom he could catch. There he devoured them at his leisure, and since he was the only person who could force a passage through the wood nobody had been able to pursue him.

While the prince was wondering what to believe, an old peasant took up the tale.

"Your Highness," said he, "more than fifty years ago I heard my father say that in this castle lies a princess, the most beautiful that has ever been seen. It is her doom to sleep there for a hundred years, and then to be awakened by a king's son, for whose coming she waits."

This story fired the young prince. He jumped immediately to the conclusion that it was for him to see so gay an adventure through, and impelled alike by the wish for love and glory, he resolved to set about it on the spot.

Hardly had he taken a step towards the wood when the tall trees, the brambles and the thorns, separated of themselves and made a path for him. He turned in the direction of the castle, and espied it at the end of a long avenue. This avenue he entered, and was surprised to notice that the trees closed up again as soon as he had passed, so that none of his retinue were able to follow him. A young and gallant prince is always brave, however; so he continued on his way, and presently reached a large forecourt.

The sight that now met his gaze was enough to fill him with an icy fear. The silence of the place was dreadful, and death seemed all about him. The recumbent figures of men and animals had all the appearance of being lifeless, until he perceived by the pimply noses and ruddy faces of the porters that they merely slept. It was plain, too, from their glasses, in which were still some dregs of wine, that they had fallen asleep while drinking.

The prince made his way into a great courtyard, paved with marble, and mounting the staircase entered the guardroom. Here the guards were lined up on either side in two ranks, their muskets on their shoulders, snoring their hardest. Through several apartments crowded with ladies and gentlemen in waiting, some seated, some standing, but all asleep, he pushed on, and so came at last to a chamber which was decked all over with gold. There he encountered the most beautiful sight he had ever seen. Reclining upon a bed, the curtains of which on every side were drawn back, was a princess of seemingly some fifteen or sixteen summers, whose radiant beauty had an almost unearthly luster.

Trembling in his admiration he drew near and went on his knees beside her. At the same moment, the hour of disenchantment having come, the princess awoke, and bestowed upon him a look more tender than a first glance might seem to warrant.

"Is it you, dear prince?" she said; "you have been long in coming!"

Charmed by these words, and especially by the manner in which they were said, the prince scarcely knew how to express his delight and gratification. He declared that he loved her better than he loved himself. His words were faltering, but they pleased the more for that. The less there is of eloquence, the more there is of love.

Her embarrassment was less than his, and that is not to be wondered at, since she had had time to think of what she would say to him. It seems (although the story says nothing about it) that the good fairy had beguiled her long slumber with pleasant dreams. To be brief, after four hours of talking they had not succeeded in uttering one half of the things they had to say to each other.

Now the whole palace had awakened with the princess. Every one went about his business, and since they were not all in love they presently began to feel mortally hungry. The lady-in-waiting, who was suffering like the rest, at length lost patience, and in a loud voice called out to the princess that supper was served.

The princess was already fully dressed, and in most magnificent style. As he helped her to rise, the prince refrained from telling her that her clothes, with the straight collar which she wore, were like those to which his grandmother had been accustomed. And in truth, they in no way detracted from her beauty.

They passed into an apartment hung with mirrors, and were there served with supper by the stewards of the household, while the fiddles and oboes played some old music and played it remarkably well, considering they had not played at all for just upon a hundred years. A little later, when supper was over, the chaplain married them in the castle chapel, and in due course, attended by the courtiers in waiting, they retired to rest...

*Written by*
*Charles Perrault (1628-1703)*

*Translated by*
*A.E. Johnson (1921)*

# V.

# The Fairy Garden

*(Le Jardin Féerique)*

Maurice Ravel

# V.
# The Fairy Garden

MAURICE RAVEL

1
2 Flts.
2 Cls.
EH.
Vlns. 1
Vlns. 2
Vlas.
Ces.
Bss.
Pno.
1°
p
pp
prominent
8
9
10
11
12
13
14
15

2 Flts.
a2
Ob.
EH.
2 Cls.
2 Bsns.
2 FHs.
Harp
Vln.
Solo
Vlns. 1
div.
Vlns. 2
div.
Vlas.
div.
Ces.
Bss.
pizz.
Pno.
16
17
18
19
20
21
22

2
2 Flts.
Ob.
EH.
2 Cls.
2 Bsns.
2 FHs.
Trg.
Cel.
Harp
Vln. Solo
Vlns. 1
Vlns. 2
Vla. Solo
Vlas.
Ces.
Bss.
Pno.
pp
mf
pp molto espressivo
mf espressivo
espressivo
8
23
24
25
26
27
28

3
2 Flts.
Ob.
EH.
2 Cls.
2 Bsns.
2 FHs.
Cel.
Harp
on the fingerboard
normal
pizz.
Vln. Solo
Vlns. 1
Vlns. 2
Vla. Solo
Vlas.
Ces.
Bss.
Pno.
29
30
31
32
33
34
35

4 Ritenuto
A Tempo
2 Flts.
Ob.
EH.
2 Cls.
2 Bsns.
2 FHs.
Cel.
Harp
Ritenuto
A Tempo
Vln. Solo
Vlns. 1
Vlns. 2
Vlas.
Ces.
Bss.
Pno.
arco
Tutti arco
pizz.
div.
unis.
div. arco
arpeggiate as little as possible
36
37
38
39
40
41

2 Flts.
Ob.
EH.
2 Cls.
2 Bsns.
2 FHs.
Timp.
Cym.
with mallets
Cel.
Harp
Tutti
div.
Vlns. 1
Vlns. 2
unis.
Vlas.
Ces.
Bss.
poco cresc.
m.g.
Pno.
42
43
44
45
46
47
48
49

5
2 Flts.
Ob.
EH.
2 Cls.
2 Bsns.
2 FHs.
Timp.
Trg.
Cym.
Glock.
Cel.
Harp
Vlns. 1
Vlns. 2
Vlas.
Ces.
Bss.
Pno.
ff
f
glissando
unis. pizz.
50
51
52

2 Flts.
Ob.
EH.
2 Cls.
2 Bsns.
2 FHs.
Timp.
Trg.
Cym.
Glock.
Cel.
Harp
Vlns. 1
Vlns. 2
Vlas.
arco
Ces.
unis.
Bss.
m.d.
Pno.
53
54
55
56

# Practical Analysis

## The Fairy Garden

Dramatically, the prince approaches the sleeping princess who's been under a 100-year curse. To get to the sleeping princess, he's moved through people within the bramble-covered castle who have been frozen in place for a hundred years, too. Seeing the princess, he immediately falls in love. Sensing love, the princess awakens. Later in the story the couple marry.

So dramatically, we have the prince approaching the princess, recognition of love, and a section that I'm labeling, *"And They Lived Happily Ever After."*

### Orchestral Setup

2 Flutes
1 Oboe
1 English horn
2 Bb Clarinets
2 Bassoons
2 French Horns
Timpani
Triangle
Cymbal
Glockenspiel with Keyboard

Celeste
Harp
Solo Violin
Solo Viola
Violins 1
Violins 2
Violas
Cellos
Basses

In looking at the orchestra, for a happily ever after approach, observe the lack of brass. Only two French horns are used. No trumpets, no trombones, no tuba, and only half the standard French horn section. Yet, despite this brass absence, Ravel's voicing of the fanfare performed by the orchestra's woodwind ensemble, is still full, rich, and emotionally satisfying. Despite the absence of brass, there's no question musically that the prince and the princess, upon entering the fairy garden, lived happily ever after.

## Form by Orchestration

As with other of the Mother Goose Suites we've looked at, Ravel has multiple structures happening simultaneously. What struck me in going through the score is that there's clearly a form of orchestration in this piece.

**Bars 1 - 22** = Largely string ensemble written within the context of a 4-part chorale.

**Bars 23 - 39** = Large melody and background line. The melody is carried by solo Violin, in places doubled by a solo Viola an octave below, with five- and seven-part harmony in the Harp. The woodwinds do not exactly "double" the Harp part. What Ravel does is to carve out a separate background line from the harmony, but in the upper register. The Bassoons are tacit until bar 31.

**Bars 40 - 49** = The full ensemble with rising emotion. As emotion rises, the orchestra is anchored with a pastoral pedal point in the Basses doubled by the Bassoons. Starting in Bar 44, French horns sound "wedding bells."

**Bars 50 - 56** = I call this *Fireworks, (Happily Ever After)*. One senses the gates to the garden opening as the couple goes through.

Agreeably, this is a rather unique form analysis, but dramatically, I think it holds up.

## Melody and the 8 Keys of Professional Orchestration

For most of the pieces, Ravel has kept the melody with a solo instrument. With the final movement, we have a change in that *The Fairy Garden* is much more an "ensemble" work. So rather than seeing solo instruments carry the melody, we find sections carrying the melody, solo instruments, solo instruments in octaves, melody in multiple octaves. We also see an extensive use of divisi in the strings which merits our attention.

Below, the + sign means *unison* while the – sign means *octaves*

| Bar Numbers | Instrument(s) | Which of the 8 Keys | Dynamics |
|---|---|---|---|
| 1 - 13 | Vlns 1 (ensemble) | First Key | *pp* |
| 14 | Vlas + Cl 1 | Third Key | *pp* |
| 15 | Cellos | First Key | *pp* |
| 16 - 17 | Vlas + EH | Third Key | *pp* |
| 18 - 19 | Solo Vln + Vlns 1 + 2 Flts | Third Key | *p* |
| 20 - 22 | Ensemble Divisi Strings doubled by woodwinds | Fifth Key | *p* |
| 23 - 26 | Solo Vln + Celeste | Third Key | *pp to mf* |

| Bar Numbers | Instrument(s) | Which of the 8 Keys | Dynamics |
|---|---|---|---|
| 27 - 28 | Solo Vln + Celeste - Solo Vla | Third Key | *mf* |
| 29 - 30 | Solo Vln + Celeste | Third Key | *p* |
| 31 - 32 | Solo Viola | First Key | *p* |
| 33 - 34 | Solo Vln + Celeste - Solo Vla + Celeste | Third Key | *pp* |
| 35 | Solo Vln + Celeste - EH + Celeste | Third Key | *mf* |
| 36 - 37 | Flt 1 + Oboe 1 | Third Key | *f* |
| 38 | Violins 2 | First Key | *mf* |
| 39 | Solo Vln + Vlns 1 | Second Key | *pp* |
| 40 - 41 | Solo Vln + ½ Vlns 1 + Flt 1 - ½ Vlns 1 + Flt 2 - ½ Cellos | Third Key | *pp* |
| 42 | ½ Vlns 1 - ½ Vlns 1 - ½ Cellos | Second Key | *pp* |
| 43 | ½ Vlns 1 - ½ Vlns 1 | Second Key | *p* |
| 44 - 45 | Vlas + Flt 1 | Third Key | *p* |
| 46 | Vlns 2 + Flt 1 - Cellos + Oboe | Third Key | *mf* |
| 47 | ½ Vlns 2 + Flt 1 - Oboe | Third Key | *mf* |
| 48 | ½ Vlns 1 + Flt 1 + Celeste - ½ Vlns 2 + Oboe + Celeste - ½ Cellos + EH | Third Key | *f* |
| 49 | ½ Vlns 1 + Celeste - ½ Vlns 1 + Celeste - ½ Cellos + EH | Third Key | *f* |
| 50 - 56 | Expanded Woodwind Ensemble | Fourth Key | *ff* |

## Dynamic Range

The final piece has a full dynamic range from *pp* to *ff*, and as such, makes greater use of doubling than other movements have.

## Analysis Comments

As you can see by the 8 Keys Chart above, beginning at bar 14, there are changes to the orchestration every 1 - 2 bars. Rather than bog you down with a lot of verbiage, I'm taking a more overview in this section where I'll be referring you back to the optional color coded PDF. To get the most out of this section, my advice is to listen to the audio, then listen again with the color coded PDF so that you can follow Ravel's brilliant, but extremely subtle changes in color that move very quickly.

## Bars 1 - 22

As a jazz major, I was excited to go through this section, because for me, it was line writing ala Ravel. Anyone fluent in jazz and chord scales should study this passage closely to see how to apply "jazz harmony" in a chorale-like setting for strings. Let me get you started. The first chord tells the story. I read it as a CMAJ7$^{ADD9}$. Breaking classical tradition, the seventh degree in the alto voice is unprepared. The D in beat 2 is the ninth of the C chord.

Go to bars 2 - 3. Look carefully at the melody, then look at the bass line. The bass line is going in contrary motion to the melody! So here Ravel applies a classical principle. Now look at the chords. In bar 2, following traditional harmonic practice, Ravel would get an F because the bass line and the harmony combined are all dissonances. D - E is a ninth. E - D is a seventh. F - G is a ninth. When you work out the chord progression for bar 2, it's DMIN$^{ADD9}$, EMIN7, and an F$^{ADD9}$.

This is a very contemporary harmonization of a melodic line, still contemporary sounding in the early $21^{st}$ Century. While often the melody is a tone from a triad, Ravel harmonizes the melody so that the tones are the seventh or ninth of the chord.

Look at bar 6. Some might say this is polytonality with a BMIN/E going to an EMIN. Or, you could say, from a jazz harmony perspective, that this is EMIN7$^{ADD9}$. At Berklee, we would call the BMIN an upper structure triad. We would also note what jazzers call "modal interchange." The EMIN with the added ninth (F#) is "borrowed" from G, even though it's iii in C. The chord scale here is E Aeolian.

Now, I'm not doing a complete harmonic analysis here, because I can't think of anything more boring to read. However, I've put you in a direction on this, and there are a few things I'll point out harmonically in the score as we go along.

**String Ensemble.** In this section, Ravel starts with Violins 1, Violins 2, Violas and Cellos. No Basses. The result is a very warm intimate sound. At bar 14, the ensemble changes. You now have Violins 2, Violas, Cellos and Basses. That runs through bar 17.

**5 notes.** Look at bars 9, 11, 12, and 13. Up until these bars, it's been a simple four-part structure. Now, looking at the Piano part, a fifth harmonic part is added. With a Piano, or with an electronic scoring setup, the extra harmony is no problem. Just play it. In the orchestra, it's a problem in the strings, because adding that extra harmony part can affect balance, depending on how it's handled.

We know from reading the earlier chapter *How Ravel Worked* that Ravel brought in a violinist to work out the bowings. So, and this is up to the concert master and conductor at time of live performance, the harmony in Violins 2 is an easy double stop. Or, they may elect to divide the strings. Notice that there's no marking for divisi in the score.

Look at bar 13 in the Piano and the Violas. To create a more open harmony, Ravel revoices the triad so that the "extra" pitch is also handled as a double stop.

**Transition to 14.** This is very subtle. In the Piano part at 12 - 13, the high G sustains in both bars. Look for the high G in Violins 1. Violins 2 lead into it, Violins 1 drop out and Violins 2 sustain in their place. At the beginning of beat 2, Violins 2 fade out, but to continue the sustain, Ravel brings in Flute 1. This sets up a subtle change and transition to bar 14. Look at the colorized score and follow the transition of the melody from Violas to Basses and how Clarinet 1 supports the Violas then moves up to an inner moving line.

Starting at 14, watch the use of imitation with the melodic theme and how its use builds intensity.

**Bars 19 - 22.** Starting at 19 Ravel builds to an emotional high point that transitions, but observe that the whole orchestra is playing, the strings are divided, and the woodwinds and French horns are doubling the strings. At 19, the melodic theme moves to Violins 2 who are divided in octaves for one bar. The upper line of Violins 2 is doubled by the Oboe while the lower part is doubled by Clarinet 2.

Look at bar 20 in the Piano, bass clef. The left hand is voiced with a common root - fifth - third voicing. In film scoring, two ways to score that voicing, working from the bottom up, are: Basses - Cellos B - Cellos A; or Basses, Cellos, Violas. Here, Ravel does neither. The bottom pitch is performed pizzicato in the Basses. The Cellos perform the root and fifth as an easy double stop doubled by the Bassoons. The third of the chord is performed by 1/2 of the Violas (double stopped) and French horn 2.

Look at the Piano part's treble clef. You see a triad in four part harmony. The melody is now in the top line of Violins 1 plus the solo Violin. Violins 1 are divided, as are Violins 2, but notice that Violins 2 have three pitches to perform. The Violas have four pitches!

Violins 1 are clearly divided.

Violins 2 are clearly divided, but 1/2 Violins 2 play a single line while the other half perform with double stops. The melody is doubled in Violins 2B an octave below Violins 1.

As you work your way down through the strings, what Ravel has done is to double the melody and harmony in triads in multiple octaves so that unlike the Piano part, the middle register is also covered.

| | |
|---|---|
| **Melody** | Solo Violin + ½ Violins 1 + Flute 1 |
| **Harmony** | ½ Violins 1 + Flute 2 |
| **Harmony** | ½ Violins 2 + Clarinet 1 |

| | |
|---|---|
| **Melody** | ½ Violins 2 + Oboe |
| **Harmony** | ½ Violins 2 |
| **Harmony** | ½ Violas |
| | |
| **Melody** | ½ Violas + French horn 1 |
| **Harmony** | ½ Violas + Clarinet 2 |
| **Harmony** | ½ Violas + French horn 2 |

The dynamic here is *p*. Notice that different colors are on the melody. The woodwinds are voiced Flt 1 - Flt 2 - Clarinet 1. The Clarinet is placed in the register where it has its most flute-like qualities. The melody is next on the Oboe an octave below. An octave below the Oboe is French horn 1. Here the triad is voiced French horn 1 - Clarinet 2 - French horn 2.

This is where, on your optional blank PDF copy of the score, you should first mark the Violins so you know roughly how many players per part. Then look at how and where Ravel doubled the woodwinds and strings. If you have any method of electronic scoring, transpose the Clarinet, French horn and English horn parts to concert pitch and then sequence bars 18 - 22. Here you'll discover the mixing of timbres in every instrument perfectly selected for the register the parts appear in.

At 21-22, the Harp catches the inner line in the Piano part to set up the next section.

## Bars 23 - 39

Dramatically, this could be an example of sweetness, or more practically, the answer to the producer's question, "So...what do fairies sound like musically?" Here's a potential answer.

Look at the Piano part. Ravel indicates an arpeggio, creating a kind of strummed effect. Yet, with the harp, there's no such indication. All the parts are "plucked" in time. No "strumming" effect at all. The dynamic is *pp*. Only the upper register part of the Harp is doubled by the woodwinds, and they must play softly enough to blend with the Harp.

The solo Violin plays the melody, later, reinforced an octave below by the solo Violist. In a live performance, to get the woodwinds and harp to blend at this dynamic level and in the high and very high registers of the Flute, is very, very demanding. This requires precision performance.

## Bars 40 - 49

Dramatically, I would define this section as: resolution, my dream come true, I've found my love at last. From 36 - 39, you have a building in the strings only to set up this section. At bar 40, the flutes in octave double Violins 1 divisi in octaves and then drop out. This incredibly subtle and deft bit of scoring really sets up the soli string ensemble. Starting at bar 40, the melody is in three octaves: Violins 1A - Violins 1B - Cellos A. Violins 2 and Violas are also divisi and play the inner triadic parts.

In the Piano, we see the root - fifth - third voicing, which Ravel orchestrates directly with Basses A on the root, Basses B on the fifth, and Cellos B on the third.

Starting at bar 44, look at 44, 46 and 48 and see how using imitation at the octave, Ravel builds the intensity with the melody ultimately playing over three octaves: Violins 1A - Violins 2B - Cellos (then in 49, Cellos A). In the woodwinds, this is doubled by Flute 1 - Oboe - English horn, also in octaves.

From 44 - 49 in the French horns, a wedding bell effect can be heard with only French horn 2. From 50 on, both French horns would play the wedding bell part doubled by pizzicato Cellos.

For a film, this would not be handled so subtlety. More than likely, depending on the size of the orchestra, you'd have at least two French horns on the part, and most likely, the bells would be up.

Also from 44 - 49 is a pastoral pedal point (root and fifth sounded simultaneously) that's sustained in the Basses, doubled by the Harp and Bassoons (which are not sustained).

From 48 - 49 Ravel uses the Celeste playing triads in both hands (which doubles both the strings and woodwinds) to set up the actual entrance into the Fairy Garden, where the couple will live happily every after.

## Bars 50 - 56: *And They Lived Happily Ever After*

The orchestra is at *ff*. The pastoral pedal point changes to a C tonality.

The melody is in the Flutes in thirds + Glockenspiel, doubled an octave below by the Clarinets + Oboe 1, and both French horns on beat 1.

The woodwinds are largely doubled by Violins 1 and Violins 2 playing fingered tremolo.

Compare the Piano part to see how Ravel handled the glisses in the Celeste and Harp.

Now, whether you look at this as *"happily ever after"* or *fireworks*, what you have to realize is that the finger tremolo Strings + Harp glisses + Celeste glisses + Glockenspiel is one giant orchestral effect. It's a blend where no part really stands out on its own independently. Add into this blend the trilled cymbal and triangle.

Bars 53 - 56 have the complete woodwind ensemble playing the fanfare. In the Piano part, Ravel voices the fanfare in triads, but in the score, Ravel learns from Bizet and voices the fanfare as thirds in octaves.

## Electronic Scoring Considerations

Up through bar 19, this is relatively easy to execute. Starting at bar 20 we have a tutti orchestra and divided strings at a dynamic of *p*. Care should be taken with divided strings and blending the woodwinds so that neither section is overpowered.

From 23 - 39, the Harp part will need to be sequenced on two tracks. The Celeste sounds an octave higher than is written and care should be taken to see that it doesn't overpower the solo Violin and solo Viola.

From 40 - 49, Ravel has divided strings and significant editing may be needed to maintain balance.

From 50 - 56, at this point in the technology, very few libraries have fingerboard tremolo, so this will have to be performed manually. Glisses in the Harp and Celeste must not be quantized or they will sound mechanical. The woodwinds plus French horn must be blended properly.

# Putting To Work What You've Learned

I'm concluding our time by looking at some general writing principles we learned from Ravel that can be applied to most any style of music. Take these points seriously and apply them whenever you write.

## Learn to Work the Melody

By this I mean, look to see within your own melodic lines the ebbs and flows, the high points and the low points. What type of harmony is needed to express your intent, especially in critical dramatic places in the melodic line?

We've seen several examples of Ravel using different kinds of background lines and accompaniments at different points in the melody. As you begin to sketch and arrange your melody, imitate Ravel. It's easy enough to keep to one or two rhythmic patterns throughout the song, but to see what kind of background is needed in different sections of the melody requires thought, imagination, and experimentation. In other words, it takes time. In a time crunched situation, this isn't always possible. But when it is, allow yourself the time to test and experiment.

Where there's a bass line, the bass doesn't have to be the instrument that performs it. In *Mother Goose Suite*, we've seen the Cellos, Timpani and Harp on the bass line in different movements. So don't be afraid to experiment.

## Ask Questions & For Musicians to Perform Parts of Your Composition

Ravel didn't learn things "cosmically." He had two main mentors, Gabriel Faure, and the great counterpoint teacher, Andre Gedalge who directly influenced his orchestration. But as you read in the earlier section, *How Ravel Worked*, he asked questions. To make sure a part was playable, he'd go to the musician's home and ask him to perform it and critique it. For his string bowings, and potential fingerings, he brought in a concert violinist to mark the parts for him.

## Learn to Apply Counterpoint

Using academic language, you can see Ravel's use of Species 1 - 4 Counterpoint, contrary motion, imitation, and in *Little Ugly*, the use of a canon. These are all tools, and nothing Ravel wrote sounded academic at all! That's because Ravel applied the principles of counterpoint, not academic rules. Ravel knew how to write counterpoint in each of the modes. For a full treatment of this, please see my text, *Counterpoint by Fux*, and the online study series, *The Instant Composer: Counterpoint by Fux*, which makes counterpoint accessible and applicable for most musical situations.

## A Note to "Jazzers"

Too often we've looked at jazz harmony as something for jazz and jazz only. Yet, what we learn from Ravel is that he absorbed this harmonic language and could write with it in such a way that nearly 100 years after this work was composed, it still sounds fresh and contemporary to our ears. Ravel's challenge to those of us who've come out of a jazz background, is to take our harmonic language and apply it beyond the scope of the small group or the big band.

## To Those Who Would Write for Film, TV, the Stage or the Internet

In this work, there are many dramatic colors, and many techniques we've heard used in the works of many famous film composers. *Mother Goose Suite*, and works like this, are the source of film composing techniques. Did you know that in *Jaws*, John Williams wrote a fugue that was performed in the movie? Did you know that the flute solo register used by Ravel in *Little Ugly* is the register where Jerry Goldsmith wrote the majority of his flute solos? Did you notice the emotion raised by moving the string ensemble up without the basses? John Williams uses this all the time. All of these dramatic "film scoring" techniques are here, but notice that they originated in the concert hall and in the ballet before there was ever film. Your challenge is to see how to make them your own.

## It's a Wrap

It is now 2:18AM Eastern Time, October 10, 2008. Read, learn, apply.

Goodnight.

# The Philosophy Of Composition

## By Edgar Allan Poe

Charles Dickens, in a note now lying before me, alluding to an examination I once made of the mechanism of "Barnaby Rudge," says — "By the way, are you aware that Godwin wrote his 'Caleb Williams' backwards? He first involved his hero in a web of difficulties, forming the second volume, and then, for the first, cast about him for some mode of accounting for what had been done."

I cannot think this the precise mode of procedure on the part of Godwin — and indeed what he himself acknowledges, is not altogether in accordance with Mr. Dickens' idea — but the author of "Caleb William" was too good an artist not to perceive the advantage derivable from at least a somewhat similar process. Nothing is more clear than that every plot, worth the name, must be elaborated to its dénouement before any thing be attempted with the pen. It is only with the dénouement constantly in view that we can give a plot its indispensable air of consequence, or causation, by making the incidents, and especially the tone at all points, tend to the development of the intention.

There is a radical error, I think, in the usual mode of constructing a story. Either history affords a thesis — or one is suggested by an incident of the day — or, at best, the author sets himself to work in the combination of striking events to form merely the basis of his narrative — designing, generally, to fill in with description, dialogue, or autorial comment, whatever crevices of fact, or action, may, from page to page, render themselves apparent.

I prefer commencing with the consideration of an effect. Keeping originality always in view — for he is false to himself who ventures to dispense with so obvious and so easily attainable a source of interest — I say to myself, in the first place, "Of the innumerable effects, or impressions, of which the heart, the intellect, or (more generally) the soul is susceptible, what one shall I, on the present occasion, select?" Having chosen a novel, first, and secondly a vivid effect, I consider whether it can best be wrought by incident or tone — whether by ordinary incidents and peculiar tone, or the converse, or by peculiarity both of incident and tone — afterward looking about me (or rather within) for such combinations of event, or tone, as shall best aid me in the construction of the effect.

I have often thought how interesting a magazine paper might be written by any author who would — that is to say, who could — detail, step by step, the processes by which any one of his compositions attained its ultimate point of completion. Why such a paper has never been given to the world, I am much at a loss to say — but, perhaps, the autorial vanity has had more to do with the omission than any one other cause. Most writers — poets in especial — prefer having it understood that they compose by a species of fine frenzy — an ecstatic intuition — and would positively shudder at letting the public take a peep behind the scenes, at the elaborate and vacillating crudities of thought — at the true purposes seized only at the last moment — at the innumerable glimpses of idea that arrived not at the maturity of full view — at the fully matured fancies discarded in despair as unmanageable — at the cautious selections and rejections — at the painful erasures and interpolations — in a word, at the wheels and pinions — the tackle for scene-shifting — the step-ladders, and demon-traps — the cock's feathers, the red paint and the black patches, which, in ninety-nine cases out of the hundred, constitute the properties of the literary histrio.

I am aware, on the other hand, that the case is by no means common, in which an author is at all in condition to retrace the steps by which his conclusions have been attained. In general, suggestions, having arisen pell-mell, are pursued and forgotten in a similar manner.

For my own part, I have neither sympathy with the repugnance alluded to, nor, at any time, the least difficulty in recalling to mind the progressive steps of any of my compositions; and, since the interest of an analysis, or reconstruction, such as I have considered a desideratum, is quite independent of any real or fancied interest in the thing analyzed, it will not be regarded as a breach of decorum on my part to show the modus operandi by which some one of my own works was put together. I select "The Raven" as most generally known. It is my design to render it manifest that no one point in its composition is referable either to accident or intuition — that the work proceeded step by step, to its completion with the precision and rigid consequence of a mathematical problem.

Let us dismiss, as irrelevant to the poem per se, the circumstance — or say the necessity — which, in the first place, gave rise to the intention of composing a poem that should suit at once the popular and the critical taste.

We commence, then, with this intention.

The initial consideration was that of extent. If any literary work is too long to be read at one sitting, we must be content to dispense with the immensely important effect derivable from unity of impression — for, if two sittings be required, the affairs of the world interfere, and every thing like totality is at once destroyed. But since, *ceteris paribus*, no poet can afford to dispense with any thing that may advance his design, it but remains to be seen whether there is, in extent, any advantage to counterbalance the loss of unity which attends it. Here I say no, at once. What we term a long poem is, in fact, merely a succession of brief ones — that is to say, of brief poetical effects. It is needless to demonstrate that a poem is such, only inasmuch as it intensely excites, by elevating the soul; and all intense excitements are, through a psychal necessity, brief. For this reason, at least, one half of the "Paradise Lost" is essentially prose — a succession of poetical excitements interspersed, inevitably, with corresponding depressions — the whole being deprived, through the extremeness of its length, of the vastly important artistic element, totality, or unity, of effect.

It appears evident, then, that there is a distinct limit, as regards length, to all works of literary art — the limit of a single sitting — and that, although in certain classes of prose composition, such as "Robinson Crusoe," (demanding no unity), this limit may be advantageously overpassed, it can never properly be overpassed in a poem. Within this limit, the extent of a poem may be made to bear mathematical relation to its merit — in other words, to the excitement or elevation — again in other words, to the degree of the true poetical effect which it is capable of inducing; for it is clear that the brevity must be in direct ratio of the intensity of the intended effect: — this, with one proviso — that a certain degree of duration is absolutely requisite for the production of any effect at all.

Holding in view these considerations, as well as that degree of excitement which I deemed not above the popular, while not below the critical, taste, I reached at once what I conceived the proper length for my intended poem — a length of about one hundred lines. It is, in fact, a hundred and eight.

My next thought concerned the choice of an impression, or effect, to be conveyed: and here I may as well observe that, throughout the construction, I kept steadily in view the design of rendering the work universally appreciable. I should be carried too far out of my immediate topic were I to demonstrate a point upon which I have repeatedly insisted, and which, with the poetical, stands not in the slightest need of demonstration — the point, I mean, that Beauty is the sole legitimate province of the poem. A few words, however, in elucidation of my real meaning, which some of my friends have evinced a disposition to misrepresent. That pleasure which is at once the most intense, the most elevating, and the most pure, is, I believe, found in the contemplation of the beautiful. When, indeed, men speak of Beauty, they mean, precisely, not a quality, as is supposed, but an effect — they refer, in short, just to that intense and pure elevation of soul — not of intellect, or of heart — upon which I have commented, and which is experienced in consequence of contemplating "the beautiful."

Now I designate Beauty as the province of the poem, merely because it is an obvious rule of Art that effects should be made to spring from direct causes — that objects should be attained through means best adapted for their attainment — no one as yet having been weak enough to deny that the peculiar elevation alluded to, is most readily attained in the poem. Now the object, Truth, or the satisfaction of the intellect, and the object Passion, or the excitement of the heart, are, although attainable, to a certain extent, in poetry, far more readily attainable in prose. Truth, in fact, demands a precision, and Passion, a homeliness (the truly passionate will comprehend me) which are absolutely antagonistic to that Beauty which, I maintain, is the excitement, or pleasurable elevation, of the soul. It by no means follows from any thing here said, that passion, or even truth, may not be introduced, and even profitably introduced, into a poem — for they may serve in elucidation, or aid the general effect, as do discords in music, by contrast — but the true artist will always contrive, first, to tone them into proper subservience to the predominant aim, and, secondly, to enveil them, as far as possible, in that Beauty which is the atmosphere and the essence of the poem.

Regarding, then, Beauty as my province, my next question referred to the tone of its highest manifestation — and all experience has shown that this tone is one of sadness. Beauty of whatever kind, in its supreme development, invariably excites the sensitive soul to tears. Melancholy is thus the most legitimate of all the poetical tones.

The length, the province, and the tone, being thus determined, I betook myself to ordinary induction, with the view of obtaining some artistic piquancy which might serve me as a key-note in the construction of the poem — some pivot upon which the whole structure might turn. In carefully thinking over all the usual artistic effects — or more properly points, in the theatrical sense — I did not fail to perceive immediately that no one had been so universally employed as that of the refrain. The universality of its employment sufficed to assure me of its intrinsic value, and spared me the necessity of submitting it to analysis. I considered it, however, with regard to its susceptibility of improvement, and soon saw it to be in a primitive condition. As commonly used, the refrain, or burden, not only is limited to lyric verse, but depends for its impression upon the force of monotone — both in sound and thought. The pleasure is deduced solely from the sense of identity — of repetition. I resolved to diversify, and so vastly heighten, the effect, by adhering, in general, to the monotone of sound, while I continually varied that of thought: that is to say, I determined to produce continuously novel effects, by the variation of the application of the refrain — the refrain itself remaining, for the most part, unvaried.

These points being settled, I next bethought me of the nature of my refrain. Since its application was to be repeatedly varied, it was clear that the refrain itself must be brief, for there would have been an insurmountable difficulty in frequent variations of application in any sentence of length. In proportion to the brevity of the sentence, would, of course, be the facility of the variation. This led me at once to a single word as the best refrain.

The question now arose as to the character of the word. Having made up my mind to a refrain, the division of the poem into stanzas was, of course, a corollary: the refrain forming the close to each stanza. That such a close, to have force, must be sonorous and susceptible of protracted emphasis, admitted no doubt: and these considerations inevitably led me to the long 'o' as the most sonorous vowel, in connection with 'r' as the most producible consonant.

The sound of the refrain being thus determined, it became necessary to select a word embodying this sound, and at the same time in the fullest possible keeping with that melancholy which I had predetermined as the tone of the poem. In such a search it would have been absolutely impossible to overlook the word "Nevermore." In fact, it was the very first which presented itself.

The next desideratum was a pretext for the continuous use of the one word "nevermore." In observing the difficulty which I had at once found in inventing a sufficiently plausible reason for its continuous repetition, I did not fail to perceive that this difficulty arose solely from the pre-assumption that the word was to be so continuously or monotonously spoken by a human being — I did not fail to perceive, in short, that the difficulty lay in the reconciliation of this monotony with the exercise of reason on the part of the creature repeating the word. Here, then, immediately arose the idea of a non-reasoning creature capable of speech; and, very naturally, a parrot, in the first instance, suggested itself, but was superseded forthwith by a Raven, as equally capable of speech, and infinitely more in keeping with the intended tone.

I had now gone so far as the conception of a Raven — the bird of ill omen — monotonously repeating the one word, "Nevermore," at the conclusion of each stanza, in a poem of melancholy tone, and in length about one hundred lines. Now, never losing sight of the object supremeness, or perfection, at all points, I asked myself — "Of all melancholy topics, what, according to the universal understanding of mankind, is the most melancholy?" Death — was the obvious reply. "And when," I said, "is this most melancholy of topics most poetical?" From what I have already explained at some length, the answer, here also, is obvious — "When it most closely allies itself to Beauty: the death, then, of a beautiful woman is, unquestionably, the most poetical topic in the world — and equally is it beyond doubt that the lips best suited for such topic are those of a bereaved lover."

I had now to combine the two ideas, of a lover lamenting his deceased mistress and a Raven continuously repeating the word "Nevermore" — I had to combine these, bearing in mind my design of varying, at every turn, the application of the word repeated; but the only intelligible mode of such combination is that of imagining the Raven employing the word in answer to the queries of the lover. And here it was that I saw at once the opportunity afforded for the effect on which I had been depending — that is to say, the effect of the variation of application. I saw that I could make the first query propounded by the lover — the first query to which the Raven should reply "Nevermore" — that I could make this first query a commonplace one — the second less so — the third still less, and so on — until at length the lover, startled from his original nonchalance by the melancholy character of the word itself — by its frequent repetition — and by a consideration of the ominous reputation of the fowl that uttered it — is at length excited to superstition, and wildly propounds queries of a far different character — queries whose solution he has passionately at heart — propounds them half in superstition and half in that species of despair which delights in self-torture — propounds them not altogether because he believes in the prophetic or demoniac character of the bird (which, reason assures him, is merely repeating a lesson learned by rote) but because he experiences a frenzied pleasure in so modeling his questions as to receive from the expected "Nevermore" the most delicious because the most intolerable of sorrow. Perceiving the opportunity thus afforded me — or, more strictly, thus forced upon me in the progress of the construction — I first established in mind the climax, or concluding query — that to which "Nevermore" should be in the last place an answer — that in reply to which this word "Nevermore" should involve the utmost conceivable amount of sorrow and despair.

Here then the poem may be said to have its beginning — at the end, where all works of art should begin — for it was here, at this point of my preconsiderations, that I first put pen to paper in the composition of the stanza:

*"Prophet," said I, "thing of evil! prophet still if bird or devil!*
*By that heaven that bends above us — by that God we both adore,*
*Tell this soul with sorrow laden, if within the distant Aidenn,*
*It shall clasp a sainted maiden whom the angels name Lenore —*
*Clasp a rare and radiant maiden whom the angels name Lenore."*
*Quoth the raven — "Nevermore."*

I composed this stanza, at this point, first that, by establishing the climax, I might the better vary and graduate, as regards seriousness and importance, the preceding queries of the lover — and, secondly, that I might definitely settle the rhythm, the metre, and the length and general arrangement of the stanza — as well as graduate the stanzas which were to precede, so that none of them might surpass this in rhythmical effect. Had I been able, in the subsequent composition, to construct more vigorous stanzas, I should, without scruple, have purposely enfeebled them, so as not to interfere with the climacteric effect.

And here I may as well say a few words of the versification. My first object (as usual) was originality. The extent to which this has been neglected, in versification, is one of the most unaccountable things in the world. Admitting that there is little possibility of variety in mere rhythm, it is still clear that the possible varieties of metre and stanza are absolutely infinite — and yet, for centuries, no man, in verse, has ever done, or ever seemed to think of doing, an original thing. The fact is, originality (unless in minds of very unusual force) is by no means a matter, as some suppose, of impulse or intuition. In general, to be found, it must be elaborately sought, and although a positive merit of the highest class, demands in its attainment less of invention than negation.

Of course, I pretend to no originality in either the rhythm or metre of the "Raven." The former is trochaic — the latter is octameter acatalectic, alternating with heptameter catalectic repeated in the refrain of the fifth verse, and terminating with tetrameter catalectic. Less pedantically — the feet employed throughout (trochees) consist of a long syllable followed by a short: the first line of the stanza consists of eight of these feet — the second of seven and a half (in effect two-thirds) — the third of eight — the fourth of seven and a half — the fifth the same — the sixth three and a half. Now, each of these lines, taken individually, has been employed before, and what originality the "Raven" has, is in their combination into stanza; nothing even remotely approaching this combination has ever been attempted. The effect of this originality of combination is aided by other unusual, and some altogether novel effects, arising from an extension of the application of the principles of rhyme and alliteration.

The next point to be considered was the mode of bringing together the lover and the Raven — and the first branch of this consideration was the locale. For this the most natural suggestion might seem to be a forest, or the fields — but it has always appeared to me that a close circumscription of space is absolutely necessary to the effect of insulated incident: — it has the force of a frame to a picture. It has an indisputable moral power in keeping concentrated the attention, and, of course, must not be confounded with mere unity of place.

I determined, then, to place the lover in his chamber — in a chamber rendered sacred to him by memories of her who had frequented it. The room is represented as richly furnished — this in mere pursuance of the ideas I have already explained on the subject of Beauty, as the sole true poetical thesis.

The locale being thus determined, I had now to introduce the bird — and the thought of introducing him through the window, was inevitable. The idea of making the lover suppose, in the first instance, that the flapping of the wings of the bird against the shutter, is a "tapping" at the door, originated in a wish to increase, by prolonging, the reader's curiosity, and in a desire to admit the incidental effect arising from the lover's throwing open the door, finding all dark, and thence adopting the half-fancy that it was the spirit of his mistress that knocked.

I made the night tempestuous, first, to account for the Raven's seeking admission, and secondly, for the effect of contrast with the (physical) serenity within the chamber.

I made the bird alight on the bust of Pallas, also for the effect of contrast between the marble and the plumage — it being understood that the bust was absolutely suggested by the bird — the bust of Pallas being chosen, first, as most in keeping with the scholarship of the lover, and, secondly, for the sonorousness of the word, Pallas, itself.

About the middle of the poem, also, I have availed myself of the force of contrast, with a view of deepening the ultimate impression. For example, an air of the fantastic — approaching as nearly to the ludicrous as was admissible — is given to the Raven's entrance. He comes in "with many a flirt and flutter."

*Not the least obeisance made he — not a moment stopped or stayed he,*
*But with mien of lord or lady, perched above my chamber door.*

In the two stanzas which follow, the design is more obviously carried out: —

*Then this ebony bird beguiling my sad fancy into smiling*
*By the grave and stern decorum of the countenance it wore,*
*"Though thy crest be shorn and shaven thou," I said, "art sure no craven,*
*Ghastly grim and ancient Raven wandering from the nightly shore —*
*Tell me what thy lordly name is on the Night's Plutonian shore!"*
*Quoth the Raven — "Nevermore."*

—

*Much I marvelled this ungainly fowl to hear discourse so plainly,*
*Though its answer little meaning — little relevancy bore;*
*For we cannot help agreeing that no living human being*
*Ever yet was blessed with seeing bird above his chamber door —*
*Bird or beast upon the sculptured bust above his chamber door,*
*With such name as "Nevermore."*

The effect of the dénouement being thus provided for, I immediately drop the fantastic for a tone of the most profound seriousness: — this tone commencing in the stanza directly following the one last quoted, with the line,

*But the Raven, sitting lonely on that placid bust, spoke only,* etc.

From this epoch the lover no longer jests — no longer sees any thing even of the fantastic in the Raven's demeanor. He speaks of him as a "grim, ungainly, ghastly, gaunt, and ominous bird of yore," and feels the "fiery eyes" burning into his "bosom's core." This revolution of thought, or fancy, on the lover's part, is intended to induce a similar one on the part of the reader — to bring the mind into a proper frame for the dénouement — which is now brought about as rapidly and as directly as possible.

With the dénouement proper — with the Raven's reply, "Nevermore," to the lover's final demand if he shall meet his mistress in another world — the poem, in its obvious phase, that of a simple narrative, may be said to have its completion. So far, every thing is within the limits of the accountable — of the real. A raven, having learned by rote the single word, "Nevermore," and having escaped from the custody of its owner, is driven, at midnight, through the violence of a storm, to seek admission at a window from which a light still gleams — the chamber-window of a student, occupied half in poring over a volume, half in dreaming of a beloved mistress deceased. The casement being thrown open at the fluttering of the bird's wings, the bird itself perches on the most convenient seat out of the immediate reach of the student, who, amused by the incident and the oddity of the visitor's demeanor, demands of it, in jest and without looking for a reply, its name. The raven addressed, answers with its customary word, "Nevermore" — a word which finds immediate echo in the melancholy heart of the student, who, giving utterance aloud to certain thoughts suggested by the occasion, is again startled by the fowl's repetition of "Nevermore." The student now guesses the state of the case, but is impelled, as I have before explained, by the human thirst for self-torture, and in part by superstition, to propound such queries to the bird as will bring him, the lover, the most of the luxury of sorrow, through the anticipated answer, "Nevermore." With the indulgence, to the utmost extreme, of this self-torture, the narration, in what I have termed its first or obvious phase, has a natural termination, and so far there has been no overstepping of the limits of the real.

But in subjects so handled, however skillfully, or with however vivid an array of incident, there is always a certain hardness or nakedness, which repels the artistical eye. Two things are invariably required — first, some amount of complexity, or more properly, adaptation; and, secondly, some amount of suggestiveness — some under current, however indefinite of meaning. It is this latter, in especial, which imparts to a work of art so much of that richness (to borrow from colloquy a forcible term) which we are too fond of confounding with the ideal. It is the excess of the suggested meaning — it is the rendering this the upper instead of the under current of the theme — which turns into prose (and that of the very flattest kind) the so called poetry of the so called transcendentalists.

Holding these opinions, I added the two concluding stanzas of the poem — their suggestiveness being thus made to pervade all the narrative which has preceded them. The under-current of meaning is rendered first apparent in the lines —

*"Take thy beak from out my heart, and take thy form from off my door!"*
*Quoth the Raven "Nevermore!"*

It will be observed that the words, "from out my heart," involve the first metaphorical expression in the poem. They, with the answer, "Nevermore," dispose the mind to seek a moral in all that has been previously narrated. The reader begins now to regard the Raven as emblematical — but it is not until the very last line of the very last stanza, that the intention of making him emblematical of Mournful and Never-ending Remembrance is permitted distinctly to be seen:

*And the Raven, never flitting, still is sitting, still is sitting,*
*On the pallid bust of Pallas just above my chamber door;*
*And his eyes have all the seeming of a demon's that is dreaming,*
*And the lamplight o'er him streaming throws his shadow on the floor;*
*And my soul from out that shadow that lies floating on the floor*
*Shall be lifted — nevermore.*

*The Works of the Late Edgar Allan Poe, Vol. II,*
*(1850), pp. 259-270*

# The Poetic Principle
## By Edgar Allan Poe

In speaking of the Poetic Principle, I have no design to be either thorough or profound. While discussing, very much at random, the essentiality of what we call Poetry, my principal purpose will be to cite for consideration, some few of those minor English or American poems which best suit my own taste, or which, upon my own fancy, have left the most definite impression. By "minor poems" I mean, of course, poems of little length. And here, in the beginning, permit me to say a few words in regard to a somewhat peculiar principle, which, whether rightfully or wrongfully, has always had its influence in my own critical estimate of the poem. I hold that a long poem does not exist. I maintain that the phrase, "a long poem," is simply a flat contradiction in terms.

I need scarcely observe that a poem deserves its title only inasmuch as it excites, by elevating the soul. The value of the poem is in the ratio of this elevating excitement. But all excitements are, through a psychal necessity, transient. That degree of excitement which would entitle a poem to be so called at all, cannot be sustained throughout a composition of any great length. After the lapse of half an hour, at the very utmost, it flags — fails — a revulsion ensues — and then the poem is, in effect, and in fact, no longer such.

There are, no doubt, many who have found difficulty in reconciling the critical dictum that the "Paradise Lost" is to be devoutly admired throughout, with the absolute impossibility of maintaining for it, during perusal, the amount of enthusiasm which that critical dictum would demand. This great work, in fact, is to be regarded as poetical, only when, losing sight of that vital requisite in all works of Art, *Unity*, we view it merely as a series of minor poems. If, to preserve its Unity — its totality of effect or impression — we read it (as would be necessary) at a single sitting, the result is but a constant alternation of excitement and depression. After a passage of what we feel to be true poetry, there follows, inevitably, a passage of platitude which no critical prejudgment can force us to admire; but if, upon completing the work, we read it again, omitting the first book — that is to say, commencing with the second — we shall be surprised at now finding that admirable which we before condemned — that damnable which we had previously so much admired. It follows from all this that the ultimate, aggregate, or absolute effect of even the best epic under the sun, is a nullity: — and this is precisely the fact.

In regard to the Iliad, we have, if not positive proof, at least very good reason for believing it intended as a series of lyrics; but, granting the epic intention, I can say only that the work is based in an imperfect sense of art. The modem epic is, of the supposititious ancient model, but an inconsiderate and blindfold imitation. But the day of these artistic anomalies is over. If, at any time, any very long poem *were* popular in reality, which I doubt, it is at least clear that no very long poem will ever be popular again.

That the extent of a poetical work is, *ceteris paribus*, the measure of its merit, seems undoubtedly, when we thus state it, a proposition sufficiently absurd — yet we are indebted for it to the Quarterly Reviews. Surely there can be nothing in mere *size*, abstractly considered — there can be nothing in mere *bulk*, so far as a volume is concerned, which has so continuously elicited admiration from these saturnine pamphlets! A mountain, to be sure, by the mere sentiment of physical magnitude which it conveys, *does* impress us with a sense of the sublime — but no man is impressed after *this* fashion by the material grandeur of even "The Columbiad." Even the Quarterlies have not instructed us to be so impressed by it. As *yet*, they have not *insisted* on our estimating Lamartine by the cubic foot, or Pollock by the pound — but what else are we to *infer* from their continual prating about "sustained effort"? If, by "sustained effort," any little gentleman has accomplished an epic, let us frankly commend him for the effort — if this indeed be a thing commendable — but let us forbear praising the epic on the effort's account. It is to be hoped that common sense, in the time to come, will prefer deciding upon a work of Art rather by the impression it makes — by the effect it produces — than by the time it took to impress the effect, or by the amount of "sustained effort" which had been found necessary in effecting the impression. The fact is, that perseverance is one thing and genius quite another — nor can all the Quarterlies in Christendom confound them. By and by, this proposition, with many which I have been just urging, will be received as self-evident. In the meantime, by being generally condemned as falsities, they will not be essentially damaged as truths.

On the other hand, it is clear that a poem may be improperly brief. Undue brevity degenerates into mere epigrammatism. A very short poem, while now and then producing a brilliant or vivid, never produces a profound or enduring effect. There must be the steady pressing down of the stamp upon the wax. De Beranger has wrought innumerable things, pungent and spirit-stirring, but in general they have been too imponderous to stamp themselves deeply into the public attention, and thus, as so many feathers of fancy, have been blown aloft only to be whistled down the wind.

A remarkable instance of the effect of undue brevity in depressing a poem, in keeping it out of the popular view, is afforded by the following exquisite little Serenade:

*I arise from dreams of thee*
*In the first sweet sleep of night,*
*When the winds are breathing low,*
*And the stars are shining bright.*
*I arise from dreams of thee,*
*And a spirit in my feet*
*Has led me — who knows how? —*
*To thy chamber-window, sweet!*

—

*The wandering airs they faint*
*On the dark the silent stream*
*— The champak odors fail*
*Like sweet thoughts in a dream;*
*The nightingale's complaint,*
*It dies upon her heart,*
*As I must die on shine,*
*O, beloved as thou art!*

—

*O, lift me from the grass!*
*I die, I faint, I fail!*
*Let thy love in kisses rain*
*On my lips and eyelids pale.*
*My cheek is cold and white, alas!*
*My heart beats loud and fast:*
*O, press it close to shine again,*
*Where it will break at last.*

Very few perhaps are familiar with these lines — yet no less a poet than Shelley is their author. Their warm, yet delicate and ethereal imagination will be appreciated by all, but by none so thoroughly as by him who has himself arisen from sweet dreams of one beloved to bathe in the aromatic air of a southern midsummer night.

One of the finest poems by Willis — the very best in my opinion which he has ever written — has no doubt, through this same defect of undue brevity, been kept back from its proper position, not less in the critical than in the popular view: —

*The shadows lay along Broadway,*
*'Twas near the twilight-tide —*
*And slowly there a lady fair*
*Was walking in her pride.*
*Alone walk'd she; but, viewlessly,*
*Walk'd spirits at her side.*

—

*Peace charm'd the street beneath her feet,*
*And Honour charm'd the air;*
*And all astir looked kind on her,*
*And called her good as fair —*
*For all God ever gave to her*
*She kept with chary care.*

—

*She kept with care her beauties rare*
*From lovers warm and true —*
*For heart was cold to all but gold,*
*And the rich came not to woo,*
*But honor'd well her charms to sell.*
*If priests the selling do.*

—

*Now walking there was one more fair —*
*A slight girl, lily-pale;*
*And she had unseen company*
*To make the spirit quail —*
*'Twixt Want and Scorn she walk'd forlorn,*
*And nothing could avail.*

—

*No mercy now can clear her brow*
*From this world's peace to pray*
*For as love's wild prayer dissolved in air,*
*Her woman's heart gave way! —*
*But the sin forgiven by Christ in Heaven*
*By man is cursed away!*

In this composition we find it difficult to recognise the Willis who has written so many mere "verses of society." The lines are not only richly ideal, but full of energy, while they breathe an earnestness, an evident sincerity of sentiment, for which we look in vain throughout all the other works of this author.

While the epic mania, while the idea that to merit in poetry prolixity is indispensable, has for some years past been gradually dying out of the public mind, by mere dint of its own absurdity, we find it succeeded by a heresy too palpably false to be long tolerated, but one which, in the brief period it has already endured, may be said to have accomplished more in the corruption of our Poetical Literature than all its other enemies combined. I allude to the heresy of *The Didactic*. It has been assumed, tacitly and avowedly, directly and indirectly, that the ultimate object of all Poetry is Truth. Every poem, it is said, should inculcate a moral, and by this moral is the poetical merit of the work to be adjudged. We Americans especially have patronized this happy idea, and we Bostonians very especially have developed it in full. We have taken it into our heads that to write a poem simply for the poem's sake, and to acknowledge such to have been our design, would be to confess ourselves radically wanting in the true poetic dignity and force: — but the simple fact is that would we but permit ourselves to look into our own souls we should immediately there discover that under the sun there neither exists nor *can* exist any work more thoroughly dignified, more supremely noble, than this very poem, this poem *per se*, this poem which is a poem and nothing more, this poem written solely for the poem's sake.

With as deep a reverence for the True as ever inspired the bosom of man, I would nevertheless limit, in some measure, its modes of inculcation. I would limit to enforce them. I would not enfeeble them by dissipation. The demands of Truth are severe. She has no sympathy with the myrtles. All *that* which is so indispensable in Song is precisely all *that* with which *she* has nothing whatever to do. It is but making her a flaunting paradox to wreathe her in gems and flowers. In enforcing a truth we need severity rather than efflorescence of language. We must be simple, precise, terse. We must be cool, calm, unimpassioned. In a word, we must be in that mood which, as nearly as possible, is the exact converse of the poetical. *He* must be blind indeed who does not perceive the radical and chasmal difference between the truthful and the poetical modes of inculcation. He must be theory-mad beyond redemption who, in spite of these differences, shall still persist in attempting to reconcile the obstinate oils and waters of Poetry and Truth.

Dividing the world of mind into its three most immediately obvious distinctions, we have the Pure Intellect, Taste, and the Moral Sense. I place Taste in the middle, because it is just this position which in the mind it occupies. It holds intimate relations with either extreme; but from the Moral Sense is separated by so faint a difference that Aristotle has not hesitated to place some of its operations among the virtues themselves. Nevertheless we find the *offices* of the trio marked with a sufficient distinction. Just as the Intellect concerns itself with Truth, so Taste informs us of the Beautiful, while the Moral Sense is regardful of Duty. Of this latter, while Conscience teaches the obligation, and Reason the expediency, Taste contents herself with displaying the charms: — waging war upon Vice solely on the ground of her deformity — her disproportion — her animosity to the fitting, to the appropriate, to the harmonious — in a word, to Beauty.

An immortal instinct deep within the spirit of man is thus plainly a sense of the Beautiful. This it is which administers to his delight in the manifold forms, and sounds, and odors and sentiments amid which he exists. And just as the lily is repeated in the lake, or the eyes of Amaryllis in the mirror, so is the mere oral or written repetition of these forms, and sounds, and colors, and odors, and sentiments a duplicate source of delight. But this mere repetition is not poetry. He who shall simply sing, with however glowing enthusiasm, or with however vivid a truth of description, of the sights, and sounds, and odors, and colors, and sentiments which greet him in common with all mankind — he, I say, has yet failed to prove his divine title. There is still a something in the distance which he has been unable to attain.

We have still a thirst unquenchable, to allay which he has not shown us the crystal springs. This thirst belongs to the immortality of Man. It is at once a consequence and an indication of his perennial existence. It is the desire of the moth for the star. It is no mere appreciation of the Beauty before us, but a wild effort to reach the Beauty above. Inspired by an ecstatic prescience of the glories beyond the grave, we struggle by multiform combinations among the things and thoughts of Time to attain a portion of that Loveliness whose very elements perhaps appertain to eternity alone. And thus when by Poetry, or when by Music, the most entrancing of the poetic moods, we find ourselves melted into tears, we weep then, not as the Abbate Gravina supposes, through excess of pleasure, but through a certain petulant, impatient sorrow at our inability to grasp now, wholly, here on earth, at once and for ever, those divine and rapturous joys of which *through* the poem, or *through* the music, we attain to but brief and indeterminate glimpses.

The struggle to apprehend the supernal Loveliness — this struggle, on the part of souls fittingly constituted — has given to the world all *that* which it (the world) has ever been enabled at once to understand and to *feel* as poetic.

The Poetic Sentiment, of course, may develop itself in various modes — in Painting, in Sculpture, in Architecture, in the Dance — very especially in Music — and very peculiarly, and with a wide field, in the composition of the Landscape Garden. Our present theme, however, has regard only to its manifestation in words. And here let me speak briefly on the topic of rhythm. Contenting myself with the certainty that Music, in its various modes of meter, rhythm, and rhyme, is of so vast a moment in Poetry as never to be wisely rejected — is so vitally important an adjunct, that he is simply silly who declines its assistance, I will not now pause to maintain its absolute essentiality. It is in Music perhaps that the soul most nearly attains the great end for which, when inspired by the Poetic Sentiment, it struggles — the creation of supernal Beauty. It *may* be, indeed, that here this sublime end is, now and then, attained in *fact*. We are often made to feel, with a shivering delight, that from an earthly harp are stricken notes which *cannot* have been unfamiliar to the angels. And thus there can be little doubt that in the union of Poetry with Music in its popular sense, we shall find the widest field for the Poetic development. The old Bards and Minnesingers had advantages which we do not possess — and Thomas Moore, singing his own songs, was, in the most legitimate manner, perfecting them as poems.

To recapitulate then: — I would define, in brief, the Poetry of words as *The Rhythmical Creation of Beauty.* Its sole arbiter is Taste. With the Intellect or with the Conscience it has only collateral relations. Unless incidentally, it has no concern whatever either with Duty or with Truth.

A few words, however, in explanation. *That* pleasure which is at once the most pure, the most elevating, and the most intense, is derived, I maintain, from the contemplation of the Beautiful. In the contemplation of Beauty we alone find it possible to attain that pleasurable elevation, or excitement *of the soul*, which we recognize as the Poetic Sentiment, and which is so easily distinguished from Truth, which is the satisfaction of the Reason, or from Passion, which is the excitement of the heart. I make Beauty, therefore — using the word as inclusive of the sublime — I make Beauty the province of the poem, simply because it is an obvious rule of Art that effects should be made to spring as directly as possible from their causes: — no one as yet having been weak enough to deny that the peculiar elevation in question is at least *most readily* attainable in the poem. It by no means follows, however, that the incitements of Passion or the precepts of Duty, or even the lessons of Truth, may not be introduced into a poem, and with advantage; for they may subserve incidentally, in various ways, the general purposes of the work: but the true artist will always contrive to tone them down in proper subjection to that *Beauty* which is the atmosphere and the real essence of the poem.

I cannot better introduce the few poems which I shall present for your consideration, than by the citation of the Proem to Longfellow's "Waif"

*The day is done, and the darkness*
*Falls from the wings of Night,*
*As a feather is wafted downward*
*From an Eagle in his flight.*

—

*I see the lights of the village*
*Gleam through the rain and the mist,*
*And a feeling of sadness comes o'er me,*
*That my soul cannot resist;*

—

*A feeling of sadness and longing,*
*That is not akin to pain,*
*And resembles sorrow only*
*As the mist resembles the rain.*

—

*Come, read to me some poem,*
*Some simple and heartfelt lay,*
*That shall soothe this restless feeling,*
*And banish the thoughts of day.*

—

*Not from the grand old masters,*
*Not from the bards sublime,*
*Whose distant footsteps echo*
*Through the corridors of Time.*

—

*For, like strains of martial music,*
*Their mighty thoughts suggest*
*Life's endless toil and endeavour;*
*And to-night I long for rest.*

—

*Read from some humbler poet,*
*Whose songs gushed from his heart,*
*As showers from the clouds of summer,*
*Or tears from the eyelids start;*

—

*Who through long days of labor,*
*And nights devoid of ease,*
*Still heard in his soul the music*
*Of wonderful melodies.*

—

*Such songs have power to quiet*
*The restless pulse of care,*
*And come like the benediction*
*That follows after prayer.*

—

*Then read from the treasured volume*
*The poem of thy choice,*
*And lend to the rhyme of the poet*
*The beauty of thy voice.*

—

*And the night shall be filled with music,*
*And the cares that infest the day*
*Shall fold their tents like the Arabs,*
*And as silently steal away.*

With no great range of imagination, these lines have been justly admired for their delicacy of expression. Some of the images are very effective. Nothing can be better than —

*— the bards sublime,*
*Whose distant footsteps echo*
*Down the corridors of Time.*

The idea of the last quatrain is also very effective. The poem on the whole, however, is chiefly to be admired for the graceful *insouciance* of its meter, so well in accordance with the character of the sentiments, and especially for the *ease* of the general manner. This "ease" or naturalness, in a literary style, it has long been the fashion to regard as ease in appearance alone — as a point of really difficult attainment. But not so: — a natural manner is difficult only to him who should never meddle with it — to the unnatural. It is but the result of writing with the understanding, or with the instinct, that the *tone*, in composition, should always be that which the mass of mankind would adopt — and must perpetually vary, of course, with the occasion. The author who, after the fashion of "The North American Review," should be upon *all* occasions merely "quiet," must necessarily upon *many* occasions be simply silly, or stupid; and has no more right to be considered "easy" or "natural" than a Cockney exquisite, or than the sleeping Beauty in the waxworks.

Among the minor poems of Bryant, none has so much impressed me as the one which he entitles "June." I quote only a portion of it: —

*There, through the long, long summer hours,*
*The golden light should lie,*
*And thick young herbs and groups of flowers*
*Stand in their beauty by.*
*The oriole should build and tell*
*His love-tale, close beside my cell;*
*The idle butterfly*
*Should rest him there, and there be heard*
*The housewife-bee and humming bird.*

—

*And what, if cheerful shouts at noon,*
*Come, from the village sent,*
*Or songs of maids, beneath the moon,*
*With fairy laughter blent?*
*And what if, in the evening light,*
*Betrothed lovers walk in sight*
*Of my low monument?*
*I would the lovely scene around*
*Might know no sadder sight nor sound.*

—

*I know, I know I should not see*
*The season's glorious show,*
*Nor would its brightness shine for me;*
*Nor its wild music flow;*
*But if, around my place of sleep,*
*The friends I love should come to weep,*
*They might not haste to go.*
*Soft airs and song, and the light and bloom,*
*Should keep them lingering by my tomb.*

—

*These to their soften'd hearts should bear*
*The thoughts of what has been,*
*And speak of one who cannot share*
*The gladness of the scene;*
*Whose part in all the pomp that fills*
*The circuit of the summer hills,*
*Is — that his grave is green;*
*And deeply would their hearts rejoice*
*To hear again his living voice.*

The rhythmical flow here is even voluptuous — nothing could be more melodious. The poem has always affected me in a remarkable manner. The intense melancholy which seems to well up, perforce, to the surface of all the poet's cheerful sayings about his grave, we find thrilling us to the soul — while there is the truest poetic elevation in the thrill. The impression left is one of a pleasurable sadness. And if, in the remaining compositions which I shall introduce to you, there be more or less of a similar tone always apparent, let me remind you that (how or why we know not) this certain taint of sadness is inseparably connected with all the higher manifestations of true Beauty. It is, nevertheless,

*A feeling of sadness and longing*
*That is not akin to pain,*
*And resembles sorrow only*
*As the mist resembles the rain.*

The taint of which I speak is clearly perceptible even in a poem so full of brilliancy and spirit as "The Health" of Edward Coate Pinckney: —

*I fill this cup to one made up*
*Of loveliness alone,*
*A woman, of her gentle sex*
*The seeming paragon;*
*To whom the better elements*
*And kindly stars have given*
*A form so fair that, like the air,*
*'Tis less of earth than heaven.*

—

*Her every tone is music's own,*
*Like those of morning birds,*
*And something more than melody*
*Dwells ever in her words;*
*The coinage of her heart are they,*
*And from her lips each flows*
*As one may see the burden'd bee*
*Forth issue from the rose.*

*Affections are as thoughts to her,*
*The measures of her hours;*
*Her feelings have the flagrancy,*
*The freshness of young flowers;*
*And lovely passions, changing oft,*
*So fill her, she appears*
*The image of themselves by turns, —*
*The idol of past years!*

—

*Of her bright face one glance will trace*
*A picture on the brain,*
*And of her voice in echoing hearts*
*A sound must long remain;*
*But memory, such as mine of her,*
*So very much endears,*
*When death is nigh my latest sigh*
*Will not be life's, but hers.*

—

*I fill'd this cup to one made up*
*Of loveliness alone,*
*A woman, of her gentle sex*
*The seeming paragon —*
*Her health! and would on earth there stood,*
*Some more of such a frame,*
*That life might be all poetry,*
*And weariness a name.*

It was the misfortune of Mr. Pinckney to have been born too far south. Had he been a New Englander, it is probable that he would have been ranked as the first of American lyrists by that magnanimous cabal which has so long controlled the destinies of American Letters, in conducting the thing called "The North American Review." The poem just cited is especially beautiful; but the poetic elevation which it induces we must refer chiefly to our sympathy in the poet's enthusiasm. We pardon his hyperboles for the evident earnestness with which they are uttered.

It was by no means my design, however, to expatiate upon the *merits* of what I should read you. These will necessarily speak for themselves. Boccalini, in his "Advertisements from Parnassus," tells us that Zoilus once presented Apollo a very caustic criticism upon a very admirable book: — whereupon the god asked him for the beauties of the work. He replied that he only busied himself about the errors. On hearing this, Apollo, handing him a sack of unwinnowed wheat, bade him pick out *all the chaff* for his reward.

Now this fable answers very well as a hit at the critics — but I am by no means sure that the god was in the right. I am by no means certain that the true limits of the critical duty are not grossly misunderstood. Excellence, in a poem especially, may be considered in the light of an axiom, which need only be properly *put*, to become self-evident. It is *not* excellence if it requires to be demonstrated as such: — and thus to point out too particularly the merits of a work of Art, is to admit that they are *not* merits altogether.

Among the "Melodies" of Thomas Moore is one whose distinguished character as a poem proper seems to have been singularly left out of view. I allude to his lines beginning — "Come, rest in this bosom." The intense energy of their expression is not surpassed by anything in Byron. There are two of the lines in which a sentiment is conveyed that embodies the *all in all* of the divine passion of Love — a sentiment which, perhaps, has found its echo in more, and in more passionate, human hearts than any other single sentiment ever embodied in words: —

*Come, rest in this bosom, my own stricken deer*
*Though the herd have fled from thee, thy home is still here;*
*Here still is the smile, that no cloud can o'ercast,*
*And a heart and a hand all thy own to the last.*

—

*Oh! what was love made for, if 'tis not the same*
*Through joy and through torment, through glory and shame?*
*I know not, I ask not, if guilt's in that heart,*
*I but know that I love thee, whatever thou art.*

—

*Thou hast call'd me thy Angel in moments of bliss,*
*And thy Angel I'll be, 'mid the horrors of this, —*
*Through the furnace, unshrinking, thy steps to pursue,*
*And shield thee, and save thee, — or perish there too!*

It has been the fashion of late days to deny Moore Imagination, while granting him Fancy — a distinction originating with Coleridge — than whom no man more fully comprehended the great powers of Moore. The fact is, that the fancy of this poet so far predominates over all his other faculties, and over the fancy of all other men, as to have induced, very naturally, the idea that he is fanciful only. But never was there a greater mistake. Never was a grosser wrong done the fame of a true poet. In the compass of the English language I can call to mind no poem more profoundly — more weirdly imaginative, in the best sense, than the lines commencing — "I would I were by that dim lake" — which are the composition of Thomas Moore. I regret that I am unable to remember them.

One of the noblest — and, speaking of Fancy — one of the most singularly fanciful of modern poets, was Thomas Hood. His "Fair Ines" had always for me an inexpressible charm: —

*O saw ye not fair Ines?*
*She's gone into the West,*
*To dazzle when the sun is down,*
*And rob the world of rest;*
*She took our daylight with her,*
*The smiles that we love best,*
*With morning blushes on her cheek,*
*And pearls upon her breast.*

—

*O turn again, fair Ines,*
*Before the fall of night,*
*For fear the moon should shine alone,*
*And stars unrivall'd bright;*
*And blessed will the lover be*
*That walks beneath their light,*
*And breathes the love against thy cheek*
*I dare not even write!*

—

*Would I had been, fair Ines,*
*That gallant cavalier,*
*Who rode so gaily by thy side,*
*And whisper'd thee so near!*
*Were there no bonny dames at home*
*Or no true lovers here,*
*That he should cross the seas to win*
*The dearest of the dear?*

—

*I saw thee, lovely Ines,*
*Descend along the shore,*
*With bands of noble gentlemen,*
*And banners waved before;*
*And gentle youth and maidens gay,*
*And snowy plumes they wore;*
*It would have been a beauteous dream,*
*If it had been no more!*

—

*Alas, alas, fair Ines,*
*She went away with song,*
*With music waiting on her steps,*
*And shootings of the throng;*
*But some were sad and felt no mirth,*
*But only Music's wrong,*
*In sounds that sang Farewell, farewell,*
*To her you've loved so long.*

*Farewell, farewell, fair Ines,*
*That vessel never bore*
*So fair a lady on its deck,*
*Nor danced so light before, —*
*Alas for pleasure on the sea,*
*And sorrow on the shore!*
*The smile that blest one lover's heart*
*Has broken many more!*

"The Haunted House," by the same author, is one of the truest poems ever written, — one of the truest, one of the most unexceptionable, one of the most thoroughly artistic, both in its theme and in its execution. It is, moreover, powerfully ideal — imaginative. I regret that its length renders it unsuitable for the purposes of this lecture. In place of it permit me to offer the universally appreciated "Bridge of Sighs."

*One more Unfortunate,*
*Weary of breath,*
*Rashly importunate,*
*Gone to her death!*

—

*Take her up tenderly,*
*Lift her with care;*
*Fashion'd so slenderly*
*Young, and so fair!*

—

*Look at her garments*
*Clinging like cerements;*
*Whilst the wave constantly*
*Drips from her clothing;*
*Take her up instantly,*
*Loving, not loathing.*

—

*Touch her not scornfully;*
*Think of her mournfully,*
*Gently and humanly;*
*Not of the stains of her,*
*All that remains of her*
*Now is pure womanly.*

—

*Make no deep scrutiny*
*Into her mutiny*
*Rash and undutiful:*
*Past all dishonor,*
*Death has left on her*
*Only the beautiful.*

—

*Still, for all slips of hers,*
*One of Eve's family—*
*Wipe those poor lips of hers*
*Oozing so clammily.*

—

*Loop up her tresses*
*Escaped from the comb,*
*Her fair auburn tresses;*
*Whilst wonderment guesses*
*Where was her home?*

—

*Who was her father?*
*Who was her mother?*
*Had she a sister?*
*Had she a brother?*
*Or was there a dearer one*
*Still, and a nearer one*
*Yet, than all other?*
*Alas! for the rarity*
*Of Christian charity*
*Under the sun!*
*O, it was pitiful!*
*Near a whole city full,*
*Home she had none.*

—

*Sisterly, brotherly,*
*Fatherly, motherly*
*Feelings had changed:*
*Love, by harsh evidence,*
*Thrown from its eminence;*

*Even God's providence*
*Seeming estranged.*

—

*Where the lamps quiver*
*So far in the river,*
*With many a light*
*From window and casement,*
*From garret to basement,*
*She stood, with amazement,*
*Houseless by night.*

—

*The bleak wind of March*
*Made her tremble and shiver;*
*But not the dark arch,*
*Or the black flowing river:*
*Mad from life's history,*
*Glad to death's mystery,*
*Swift to be hurl'd—*
*Anywhere, anywhere*
*Out of the world!*

—

*In she plunged boldly—*
*No matter how coldly*
*The rough river ran—*
*Over the brink of it,*
*Picture it—think of it,*
*Dissolute Man!*
*Lave in it, drink of it,*
*Then, if you can!*

—

*Take her up tenderly,*
*Lift her with care;*
*Fashion'd so slenderly,*
*Young, and so fair!*

—

*Ere her limbs frigidly*
*Stiffen too rigidly,*
*Decently, kindly,*
*Smooth and compose them;*
*And her eyes, close them,*
*Staring so blindly!*

—

*Dreadfully staring*
*Thro' muddy impurity,*
*As when with the daring*
*Last look of despairing*
*Fix'd on futurity.*

—

*Perishing gloomily,*
*Spurr'd by contumely,*
*Cold inhumanity,*
*Burning insanity,*
*Into her rest.—*
*Cross her hands humbly*
*As if praying dumbly,*
*Over her breast!*

—

*Owning her weakness,*
*Her evil behavior,*
*And leaving, with meekness,*
*Her sins to her Savior!*

The vigor of this poem is no less remarkable than its pathos. The versification although carrying the fanciful to the very verge of the fantastic, is nevertheless admirably adapted to the wild insanity which is the thesis of the poem.

Among the minor poems of Lord Byron is one which has never received from the critics the praise which it undoubtedly deserves: —

*Though the day of my destiny's over,*
*And the star of my fate hath declined*
*Thy soft heart refused to discover*
*The faults which so many could find;*
*Though thy soul with my grief was acquainted,*
*It shrunk not to share it with me,*
*And the love which my spirit hath painted*
*It never hath found but in thee.*

*Then when nature around me is smiling,*
*The last smile which answers to mine,*
*I do not believe it beguiling,*
*Because it reminds me of thine;*
*And when winds are at war with the ocean,*
*As the breasts I believed in with me,*
*If their billows excite an emotion,*
*It is that they bear me from thee.*

—

*Though the rock of my last hope is shivered,*
*And its fragments are sunk in the wave,*
*Though I feel that my soul is delivered*
*To pain — it shall not be its slave.*
*There is many a pang to pursue me:*
*They may crush, but they shall not contemn —*
*They may torture, but shall not subdue me —*
*'Tis of thee that I think — not of them.*

—

*Though human, thou didst not deceive me,*
*Though woman, thou didst not forsake,*
*Though loved, thou forborest to grieve me,*
*Though slandered, thou never couldst shake, —*
*Though trusted, thou didst not disclaim me,*
*Though parted, it was not to fly,*
*Though watchful, 'twas not to defame me,*
*Nor mute, that the world might belie.*

—

*Yet I blame not the world, nor despise it,*
*Nor the war of the many with one —*
*If my soul was not fitted to prize it,*
*'Twas folly not sooner to shun:*
*And if dearly that error hath cost me,*
*And more than I once could foresee,*
*I have found that whatever it lost me,*
*It could not deprive me of thee.*

—

*From the wreck of the past, which hath perished,*
*Thus much I at least may recall,*
*It hath taught me that which I most cherished*
*Deserved to be dearest of all:*
*In the desert a fountain is springing,*
*In the wide waste there still is a tree,*
*And a bird in the solitude singing,*
*Which speaks to my spirit of thee.*

Although the rhythm here is one of the most difficult, the versification could scarcely be improved. No nobler theme ever engaged the pen of poet. It is the soul-elevating idea that no man can consider himself entitled to complain of Fate while in his adversity he still retains the unwavering love of woman.

From Alfred Tennyson, although in perfect sincerity I regard him as the noblest poet that ever lived, I have left myself time to cite only a very brief specimen. I call him, and think him the noblest of poets, not because the impressions he produces are at all times the most profound — not because the poetical excitement which he induces is at all times the most intense — but because it is at all times the most ethereal — in other words, the most elevating and most pure. No poet is so little of the earth, earthy. What I am about to read is from his last long poem, "The Princess":

*Tears, idle tears, I know not what they mean,*
*Tears from the depth of some divine despair*
*Rise in the heart, and gather to the eyes,*
*In looking on the happy Autumn fields,*
*And thinking of the days that are no more.*

—

*Fresh as the first beam glittering on a sail,*
*That brings our friends up from the underworld,*
*Sad as the last which reddens over one*
*That sinks with all we love below the verge;*
*So sad, so fresh, the days that are no more.*

—

*Ah, sad and strange as in dark summer dawns*
*The earliest pipe of half-awaken'd birds*
*To dying ears, when unto dying eyes*
*The casement slowly grows a glimmering square;*
*So sad, so strange, the days that are no more.*

—

*Dear as remember'd kisses after death,*
*And sweet as those by hopeless fancy feign'd*
*On lips that are for others; deep as love,*
*Deep as first love, and wild with all regret;*
*O Death in Life, the days that are no more.*

Thus, although in a very cursory and imperfect manner, I have endeavoured to convey to you my conception of the Poetic Principle. It has been my purpose to suggest that, while this principle itself is strictly and simply the Human Aspiration for Supernal Beauty, the manifestation of the Principle is always found in *an elevating excitement of the soul*, quite independent of that passion which is the intoxication of the Heart, or of that truth which is the satisfaction of the Reason. For in regard to passion, alas! its tendency is to degrade rather than to elevate the Soul. Love, on the contrary — Love — the true, the divine Eros — the Uranian as distinguished from the Dionnan Venus — is unquestionably the purest and truest of all poetical themes. And in regard to Truth, if, to be sure, through the attainment of a truth we are led to perceive a harmony where none was apparent before, we experience at once the true poetical effect; but this effect is referable to the harmony alone, and not in the least degree to the truth which merely served to render the harmony manifest.

We shall reach, however, more immediately a distinct conception of what the true Poetry is, by mere reference to a few of the simple elements which induce in the Poet himself the poetical effect He recognizes the ambrosia which nourishes his soul in the bright orbs that shine in Heaven — in the volutes of the flower — in the clustering of low shrubberies — in the waving of the grain-fields — in the slanting of tall eastern trees — in the blue distance of mountains — in the grouping of clouds — in the twinkling of half-hidden brooks — in the gleaming of silver rivers — in the repose of sequestered lakes — in the star-mirroring depths of lonely wells. He perceives it in the songs of birds — in the harp of Bolos — in the sighing of the night-wind — in the repining voice of the forest — in the surf that complains to the shore — in the fresh breath of the woods — in the scent of the violet — in the voluptuous perfume of the hyacinth — in the suggestive odor that comes to him at eventide from far distant undiscovered islands, over dim oceans, illimitable and unexplored. He owns it in all noble thoughts — in all unworldly motives — in all holy impulses — in all chivalrous, generous, and self-sacrificing deeds. He feels it in the beauty of woman — in the grace of her step — in the lustre of her eye — in the melody of her voice — in her soft laughter, in her sigh — in the harmony of the rustling of her robes. He deeply feels it in her winning endearments — in her burning enthusiasms — in her gentle charities — in her meek and devotional endurances — but above all — ah, far above all, he kneels to it — he worships it in the faith, in the purity, in the strength, in the altogether divine majesty — of her love.

Let me conclude by — the recitation of yet another brief poem — one very different in character from any that I have before quoted. It is by Motherwell, and is called "The Song of the Cavalier." With our modern and altogether rational ideas of the absurdity and impiety of warfare, we are not precisely in that frame of mind best adapted to sympathize with the sentiments, and thus to appreciate the real excellence of the poem. To do this fully we must identify ourselves in fancy with the soul of the old cavalier: —

*Then mounte! then mounte, brave gallants all,*
*And don your helmes amaine:*
*Deathe's couriers. Fame and Honor call*
*Us to the field againe.*
*No shrewish teares shall fill your eye*
*When the sword-hilt's in our hand, —*
*Heart-whole we'll part, and no whit sighe*

*For the fayrest of the land;*
*Let piping swaine, and craven wight,*
*Thus weepe and poling crye,*
*Our business is like men to fight,*
*And hero-like to die !*

*The Works of the Late Edgar Allan Poe*, Vol. III,
(1850), pp. 1-20

# Bibliography

Countess of D'Aulnoy, Miss Lee (Trans.), *The Fairy Tales of Madame D'Aulnoy*, 1895

Lucas Drew, *The Notation of Harmonics for Double Bass: A Guide to the Orchestral Bass Parts of Maurice Ravel in Simplified Chart Form*, Copyright © 1972 by University of Miami, originally published by University of Miami Music Publications, Coral Gables, Florida.

Rufus Wilmot Griswold, *The Works of the Late Edgar Allan Poe*, Vol. II, 1850, originally published by J.S. Redfield, Clinton Hall, Nassau-Street, New York.

Rufus Wilmot Griswold, *The Works of the Late Edgar Allan Poe*, Vol. III, 1850, originally published by J.S. Redfield, Clinton Hall, Nassau-Street, New York.

A. E. Johnson (Trans.), *Old Time Stories told by Master Charles Perrault*, 1921 originally published by Dodd, Mead & Company, New York.

Deborah Mawer (Ed), *The Cambridge Companion to Ravel*, Copyright © 2000 by Cambridge University Press, originally published by Cambridge University Press, The Edinburgh Building, Cambridge, CB2 2RU.

Olivier Messiaen, Paul Griffiths (Trans.) *Analyses of the Piano Works of Maurice Ravel*, Copyright © 2005 Olivier Messiaen, originally published by Durand, Salbert, Eshig, Paris.

Roger Nichols, *Ravel Remembered*, Copyright © 1987 by Roger Nichols, originally published by Faber and Faber Limited, 3 Queen Square London, WC1N 3AU.

Arbie Orenstein, *Ravel Man and Musician*, Copyright © 1991 by Arbie Orenstein, originally published by Dover Publications, Inc., 31 East 2nd Street, Mineola, NY 11501.

Printed in the USA
CPSIA information can be obtained
at www.ICGtesting.com
LVHW082131161023
761258LV00045B/904